"Jeez, Fallon—you're not actually hoping to stir up trouble, are you?"

"Maybe I am," she said. "Maybe I'm tired of every man I know treating me like a buddy. Maybe I want someone to look at me and realize I'm a woman, to want me as a woman."

And suddenly he got it. "You mean me," he realized. "You want *me* to see you as a woman."

She sighed as she shook her head. "No, Jamie. I think I've finally accepted that that is never going to happen."

"But I do see you as a woman," he assured her. "A genuinely warm, funny and smart woman."

"Maybe it's un-PC," she admitted. "But I don't want to be admired for my personality or my intelligence. I want to be wanted."

Jamie swallowed. "You're looking for a hookup?"

"That wouldn't be my first choice," she said. "But I've decided to open my mind up to any and all possibilities."

"A hookup should not be one of them," he told her. "You deserve better than that."

"What does the song say—we can't always get what we want, but we get what we need?"

"Don't go, Fallon." The words were out of his mouth before he realized what he was saying.

She paused with her hand on the door.

"Don't go out to the Ace tonight."

She slowly turned around, her expression carefully neutral. "Are you making me an alternate offer?" she asked.

He nodded. "Stay here. With me."

**MONTANA MAVERICKS: The Baby Bonanza—
Meet Rust Creek Falls' newest bundles of joy!**

Dear Reader,

I have two wonderful sons, both teenagers now, but they came into my life one at a time. Though the memories of those early days and sleepless nights have faded, I haven't completely forgotten how terrified and overwhelmed I felt at times, knowing that I was responsible for the care and well-being of a helpless baby (and, two years later, a toddler *and* a baby!). So while I have absolutely no practice caring for triplets, I imagined the experience would be somewhat similar to my own... times three!

But I also had a partner with whom to share the work and the worry, which Jamie Stockton—suddenly a single dad to three premature babies—does not. Thankfully, Rust Creek Falls is the kind of community where friends and neighbors are always willing to lend a hand to others in need.

Fallon O'Reilly is happy to help take care of her friend's beautiful babies—and determined to do everything she can to make sure that their first Christmas is a merry one, despite the obstacles their dad keeps putting in her path. Jamie has a lot of reasons not to look forward to the festive season, but Fallon refuses to let him dampen her holiday spirit.

As she works her magic spreading Christmas cheer around his ranch—a tree in his living room (that she made him cut down), cookies baking in his kitchen (that she enticed him to help decorate), carols playing on the radio (that he finds himself humming along with)—he realizes that his feelings have started to change. Not just about the holidays, but about the woman who's always been one of his best friends...

And if Fallon gets *her* holiday wish, she'll find a handsome Maverick—and his three adorable children—under her tree on Christmas morning.

I hope you enjoy Jamie and Fallon's story, and that all of *your* holiday wishes come true!

Brenda Harlen

The More Mavericks, the Merrier!

—

Brenda Harlen

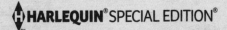
HARLEQUIN® SPECIAL EDITION®

Special thanks and acknowledgment are given to Brenda Harlen for her contribution to the Montana Mavericks: The Baby Bonanza continuity.

Recycling programs
for this product may
not exist in your area.

ISBN-13: 978-0-373-65096-5

The More Mavericks, the Merrier!

Copyright © 2016 by Harlequin Books S.A.

HARLEQUIN®
www.Harlequin.com

Printed in U.S.A.

Brenda Harlen is a former attorney who once had the privilege of appearing before the Supreme Court of Canada. The practice of law taught her a lot about the world and reinforced her determination to become a writer—because in fiction, she could promise a happy ending! Now she is an award-winning, national bestselling author of more than thirty titles for Harlequin. You can keep up-to-date with Brenda on Facebook and Twitter or through her website, brendaharlen.com.

Books by Brenda Harlen

Harlequin Special Edition

Those Engaging Garretts!

Building the Perfect Daddy
Two Doctors & a Baby
The Bachelor Takes a Bride
A Forever Kind of Family
The Daddy Wish
A Wife for One Year
The Single Dad's Second Chance
A Very Special Delivery
His Long-Lost Family
From Neighbors...to Newlyweds?

Montana Mavericks: What Happened at the Wedding?

Merry Christmas, Baby Maverick!

Montana Mavericks: 20 Years in the Saddle!

The Maverick's Thanksgiving Baby

Visit the Author Profile page
at Harlequin.com for more titles.

For Connor—it doesn't seem so very long ago that we were celebrating your first Christmas. Now you're in your first year at university, and I'm counting the days until you come home for the holidays. A lot has changed over the years, but there are two things that never will: how very proud I am to call you my son, and how much I love you. xo

Chapter One

Jamie Stockton turned the page on the calendar and stared at the letters that spelled out the month. D-E-C-E-M-B-E-R. The final month of a year that had mostly been a blur in his mind.

Twelve months earlier, he'd been anticipating the upcoming holiday and already thinking about this Christmas, when he and his wife would celebrate the holiday with their babies. Now Henry, Jared and Katie's first Christmas was only weeks away, but Paula was gone and instead of being excited about the event, he was simply exhausted.

His fingers automatically wrapped around the heavy mug that was thrust into his hand. He lifted it to his lips and swallowed a mouthful of hot, strong coffee. The caffeine slid down his throat, spread slowly through his system.

He turned away from the calendar to face his sister. "Thanks."

"You looked like you needed it," Bella said, as she started breaking eggs into a bowl.

He swallowed another mouthful of coffee. "Henry was up three times last night."

"Teething?"

"I don't know. His cheeks weren't red, he wasn't drooling and he didn't have a fever."

"Hmm." Bella turned and looked at the triplets, lined up in three high chairs beside the butcher block table, each of them focused on the cut-up pieces of fruit she'd offered to tide them over until she could cook breakfast. "He looks okay now—certainly a lot better than you do."

"Thanks," he said dryly.

She added a splash of milk and began whisking the eggs. "Did Jared and Katie sleep through the night?"

He shook his head. "Jared was awake once. Katie made it all the way through until her wet diaper woke her up at four this morning."

"And since you had to be up at five, you probably didn't even try to go back to sleep after she was changed." She poured the egg mixture into the hot pan on the stove.

"Nope," he agreed.

The truth was, even when the kids were settled in their cribs at night, sleep didn't come easily to him. When he tumbled into his own bed, unable to keep his eyes open a minute longer, his body would immediately shut down. His mind, not so much.

Although he'd always wanted to be a father, he never planned to be a single father. But that's what he was, and while the joys of being a parent to ten-month old triplets were countless, the trials were also numerous.

"I really think you should consider putting them into day care," Bella said gently.

It wasn't the first time she'd made the suggestion, and he understood that—for a lot of reasons—it was a valid one. Of course, he'd nixed the idea the first dozen times she'd mentioned it, vehemently when the town was in the midst of an RSV outbreak. But now that the epidemic had passed, maybe he would reconsider.

He nodded, because he agreed that socialization in a structured setting would be good for his children. And while the cost of day care for three babies was somewhat prohibitive, he also knew that he couldn't continue to rely on community volunteers to provide in-home care for his young family.

Since the tragic death of his wife after the birth of their babies, he'd been the grateful recipient of an outpouring of support and assistance from the residents of Rust Creek Falls. Under the direction of his sister, Bella, several volunteers had come together to create what she called a baby chain and help him take care of the triplets in rotating shifts.

For the past ten months, his sister had been the anchor of that system. Despite the demands on her, she'd somehow found the time to meet and fall in love with Hudson Jones. And Jamie knew it was time for him to take control of his own life so that she could get on with hers and the planning of her wedding.

"So you *are* thinking about day care?" she prompted, evidently surprised.

He lifted his mug again, to hide his smile behind

the rim. "I've heard a lot of great things about Country Kids."

Bella, who worked at Just Us Kids—the day care center managed by her fiancé—narrowed her gaze as she stirred the eggs in the pan.

He chuckled. "I'm kidding."

"I hope so."

"On the other hand, Fallon does work at Country Kids," he pointed out. "And they offer a discount for more than one child."

"Just Us Kids does, too," she told him, as she took the platter of bacon and toast out of the oven and set it on the table. "Plus, I'm pretty sure I can wrangle a family discount for you."

"I'm not looking for anything full-time," he told her, snagging a piece of bacon as soon as she turned her back.

"Of course not," Bella agreed, tearing a slice of toast into pieces for Henry, Jared and Katie to chew on. "Half days would be a better introduction for them. Any change in daily routine is an adjustment for a child, although the triplets do have something of an advantage in that they're accustomed to being cared for by different people."

Because they'd never had the benefit of a mother and a father to tend to their day-to-day needs, Jamie lamented silently. "That's an advantage?"

She winced. "I'm sorry. You know I didn't mean it like that."

"I know," he confirmed.

"So…half days," she said, attempting to refocus their conversation as she set a plate of eggs in front of him. "Mornings?"

He nodded as he picked up his fork to dig into his breakfast. "But not every day."

Bella sighed as she scooped smaller portions of egg into three bowls on the counter to cool off for a few minutes before she gave them to the babies. "Part-time only a few days a week isn't going to be very helpful to you when you're juggling so much," she pointed out. "You leave the house at the crack of dawn every morning, then you come back to have lunch with your kids, then you head back out to work and drop whatever you're doing to come back to check on them again in the afternoon."

"And yet I still feel guilty about relying on other people to care for them during so much of the time that they're awake," he admitted, adding a couple slices of thick, buttered toast to his plate.

She sat down with her own breakfast. "You'll feel less guilty when they're in day care—and less inclined to interrupt your day to check on them."

"Three days a week," he decided.

"Four," she countered, reaching out to snag a couple of pieces of bacon before he emptied the platter.

He scowled. "They're only ten months old."

"And I'll be at the day care every minute that they are," Bella assured him.

"I don't know," he hedged.

She didn't press any further as she finished her own breakfast, then gave the babies their eggs.

Jamie had just pushed his own plate aside when a brisk knock sounded on the back door, then Fallon O'Reilly walked into the room without waiting for an invitation.

He didn't mind. Fallon had been a friend of both

him and his sister since childhood and one of the first women to volunteer for the baby chain. She was also one of the most regular, and expediency had required that they dispense with the usual protocols months earlier.

"Good morning," Fallon greeted Jamie and Bella, her tone and her smile confirming that she believed it to be true. Then she turned to the babies, lavishly kissing each of their cheeks, making them giggle.

The sound filled his heart with joy and he looked at Fallon with sincere gratitude. She was so great with the babies—so natural and easy. She seemed to love them as he'd hoped their mother would have done, but Paula had never had the chance to be the mother he'd believed she could be—dying only hours after their babies were born by emergency C-section.

"I brought blueberry muffins." Fallon set a plastic container in the middle of the table, then moved across the kitchen to retrieve a mug from the cupboard. She brought it and the carafe to the table, offering refills to Jamie and Bella.

But Bella shook her head. "I should be getting into work."

Jamie picked up his mug and stood. "And I need to get out to the barn and check on Daisy. Brooks said she could foal any day now."

Fallon frowned at both of them. "Why are you racing off? It's barely seven-thirty."

"Hudson wants to expand Just Us Kids to offer a newborn group and I promised to help him review the applications and set up the interviews," Bella told her.

"And I've already had breakfast," Jamie said.

Fallon looked from sister to brother and back again,

her eyes narrowing. "This is about the coffee cake I made for the Fourth of July potluck, isn't it?"

Jamie and Bella exchanged a look.

Fallon huffed out an exasperated breath as she lifted the lid off the container. "I misread the recipe," she explained, selecting a muffin and peeling the paper off of the bottom half. "*Once*. And no one in this town will let me forget it."

"Because you served the cake at the potluck."

"*Three years ago*. And it wasn't really that bad," Fallon defended.

"You used two tablespoons of baking powder instead of two teaspoons," Bella reminded her, settling back in her chair. "The cake was tough and chewy."

"And tasted like metal," Jamie chimed in.

Color filled Fallon's cheeks as she tore a piece off the muffin. "Okay, it was bad," she acknowledged, as she popped the morsel into her mouth. "But these are delicious."

Jamie sat down again and reached into the container—because even after eating a full breakfast, there was room for a muffin. Bella continued to look dubious.

"I brought something else, too," Fallon said, as she broke up the bottom of the muffin into pieces and set them onto each of the babies' trays.

Henry, Jared and Kate showed no hesitation, gleefully stuffing the pieces into their mouths.

"What?" Jamie asked, nibbling tentatively on the muffin.

Fallon hesitated, not wanting to overstep. But she'd spent a lot of time with this man and his children over the past ten months, and although she understood that he was still grieving the loss of his wife, he needed to start to look forward instead of back—for the sake of his babies if no one else.

So she pulled the paper out of her pocket and unfolded it, then slid it across the table for Jamie to read.

He gave it a cursory—almost curious—glance, then looked away to focus his attention on the muffin that he suddenly couldn't shove into his mouth fast enough.

Bella leaned forward to peer at the words on the page.

"It's Henry, Jared and Katie's first Christmas," Fallon reminded Jamie gently, sliding the paper closer to him. "And I want to help you make it the best Christmas ever for them."

"They're not even a year old," he pointed out. "It's not as if they'll remember the occasion."

"Maybe not," she acknowledged. But she loved the holiday season almost as much as she loved the triplets, so she'd decided that she was going to do everything in her power to ensure that their first Christmas was a truly memorable one. That was why she'd come up with a list of suggested activities to introduce HJK—as Jamie affectionately referred to his children—to some yuletide traditions and get everyone in the holiday spirit.

Unfortunately, she knew that she would face an obstacle in their father. It was Jamie's first Christmas without his wife, and she understood it wouldn't be an easy one for him. She also believed that it wouldn't help him or his children to dwell on what they'd lost.

"But *you* will remember," Fallon told him. "And when they look back on the pictures you take over the holiday season, they'll see that you made it a wonderful one for them."

"I don't know—"

"Fallon's right," Bella interjected, reaching across the table to touch her brother's hand. "You need to do something special—for all of you. It's your first Christmas as a father—"

"And a widower," he pointed out.

"As a father," she said again, determined to emphasize the positive. "And that's a cause for celebration."

He glanced at the list again, his thick brows drawing together. "First Christmas photo with Santa? Am I supposed to ask the fat guy to pose with HJK after he squeezes down the chimney on Christmas Eve?"

"No," Fallon said, with what she thought was incredible patience. "You're supposed to take them to the mall in Kalispell."

He was shaking his head before she even finished speaking. "I don't do malls and I don't have the time—or the inclination—to bundle up three babies, strap their screaming, squirming bodies into car seats, and trek into the city to stand in line with dozens of other harried parents for a photo op with a phony Kris Kringle."

"Well, the real one is kind of busy at the North Pole this time of year," she shot back, deadpan. "And you need to make the time and fake the inclination if necessary, because this is important."

"To whom?" he countered.

"To me," Bella interjected, obviously attempting to play peacemaker. "I'd love a picture of my niece and nephews with Santa."

"Then *you* can take them," Jamie told her.

Fallon drew in a slow, deep breath and mentally counted to ten. It wouldn't help the situation if she lost her temper, but she was so frustrated with him—and for him. She knew he was grieving, but she also knew he loved his babies and, when he finally stopped grieving, he would regret the opportunities he'd missed. She wasn't going to let him have regrets.

"We'll put that one aside for now," she finally relented. "The outfits I've ordered haven't come in yet, anyway."

His frown was back again. "You ordered outfits?"

"Wait until you see them. They're the—"

"I don't want to see them," he told her. "I want you to send them back. I can afford to buy clothes for my kids. I don't need your charity."

Fallon sighed. "It's not charity. It's a gift."

"And very thoughtful," Bella interjected again, with a pointed look at her brother.

Jamie sighed. "Bella's right. I'm sorry."

"Prove it," she said.

His brows lifted. "How am I supposed to prove it?"

"By agreeing to fulfill the requirements of my list."

"I'm not *that* sorry." He pushed the paper away from him.

She shoved it at him again.

With a sigh, he reached out to take it, his fingertips brushing against hers in the transfer. Little sparks skipped through her veins in response to the brief contact.

She glanced up, to see if he'd experienced any kind of reaction. His gaze remained focused on the page, his expression neutral.

"I have no objection to a tree," he finally conceded.

Fallon ignored her own disappointment. "Great," she said. "We'll bundle the kids up this afternoon, take them in the sleigh out to the woods and find an appropriate specimen."

"That's a wonderful idea," Bella agreed.

Jamie frowned. "This afternoon? What's the hurry? It's only the first day of December."

"A tree is the most obvious symbol of Christmas," Fallon pointed out reasonably. "Having one in the house will help you get into the spirit of the season."

Nothing in his expression hinted at the tiniest bit of holiday spirit, but he shrugged. "Fine. Whatever. If you want to take the kids out and chop down a tree, I'll see if one of the kids from next door is available to help you drag it back."

"Uh-uh," Fallon said, shaking her head. "I'm not taking the kids out to chop down a tree—*we* are."

"I don't have time—"

"Make time," she said, interrupting his familiar refrain.

He frowned. "When did you get to be so bossy?"

"She's always been bossy," Bella chimed in. "I don't know how it's possible that you've known her for more than twenty years and not known that."

But Fallon wasn't surprised that he hadn't noticed her ability to take charge and assert herself when the situation warranted. There were a lot of things that Jamie had never noticed about her. Most notably the Montana-sized crush she'd had on him since she was a girl experiencing the first stirring of adolescent hormones.

And while a part of her was grateful that he'd never discovered her feelings for him, another part continued to be frustrated that he'd always viewed her as his kid sister's friend. Sure, over the years they'd developed a friendship of their own outside of their mutual connection to Bella, but Jamie had only ever seen her as a pal to hang out with and an occasional confidante.

She was the only person he'd shared his anger and frustration with when he'd discovered that his wife had secretly been taking birth control while he'd thought they were trying to get pregnant. Of course, when Paula finally had conceived, Jamie had shared the good news with everyone in Rust Creek Falls. He'd been so thrilled, he'd practically shouted it from the rooftops. But he'd subsequently admitted to Fallon that Paula wasn't nearly as excited about having a baby as he was—and even less so when they learned that she would have three of them.

"I thought you were the bossy one," Jamie responded to his sister's comment while his speculative gaze lingered on Fallon.

"I'm not bossy," she denied.

His lips twitched. "Of course not. And now, I really do need to get out to the barn to check on Daisy," he said, suddenly remembering his expectant mare.

Fallon nodded. "Will we see you at lunch?"

"Not if I'm going to finish up early to go out hunting for a Christmas tree."

"I didn't ask you to do that," she pointed out.

"It gets dark early this time of year." He snagged a couple of muffins out of the container on the table, then winked at her on his way to the door. "These will tide me over."

She started to offer to wrap them up and fill a thermos with coffee, then clenched her teeth to hold back the words. She was pleased that he liked the muffins, but while offering baked goods was an acceptable and neighborly gesture, sending him off with a bagged lunch and a hot beverage was something a wife would do.

And Fallon wasn't his wife—she was his friend and his children's babysitter, nothing more. She needed to remember that—for the sake of her own heart.

Chapter Two

While Jamie was making his way to the door, his sister started clearing the breakfast dishes off the table.

"If you have to get to work, I can take care of that," Fallon offered.

"I'm not really in a hurry," Bella admitted.

"You don't have to meet Hudson to look at applications?"

"Not until this afternoon."

Fallon shook her head. "Really? You were so afraid to sample my baking that you made up that story?"

"I didn't make it up," her friend denied. "I just fudged the timeline a little."

"I've prepared lunch and occasionally dinner here numerous times over the past ten months and you never balked at eating anything I've cooked," she pointed out.

"You know how to put a meal together," Bella confirmed. "Dessert? Not so much."

"Ouch."

"You have a lot of talents," her friend soothed. "Baking just isn't one of them."

"But the muffins were good, weren't they?"

"They were very good, but one batch of muffins isn't going to make anyone forget the potluck experience."

Fallon scowled as she washed the babies' hands and faces, then she and Bella carried the triplets into the living room.

Because Henry, Jared and Katie were preemies—born almost two months ahead of schedule—they were a little bit delayed in their development and had only recently started to crawl and climb. Their sudden mobility had Jamie in a panic about childproofing the house, so there were now caps in all of the outlets, child locks and latches on all of the doors and drawers and baby gates to block off the rooms that were completely off-limits to the little ones.

He also had a play yard—which Fallon thought was intended to go *in* the yard, but he'd assured her was also suitable for indoor use and gave the babies a little more room to roam around than a traditional playpen. But for now, with Bella there to provide an extra set of eyes, they were letting the babies crawl around the floor.

While her brothers were playing with wooden toy cars, Katie was preoccupied with the sparkly ring on Bella's finger. "Pretty, isn't it?" Fallon said.

Katie, of course, didn't respond but continued to be mesmerized by the massive diamond.

"You're a smart girl," her Auntie Bella said. "You already know that diamonds are a girl's best friend."

"And her brothers are already obsessed with cars," Fallon noted.

"Whatever keeps them busy…and happy," Bella said, smiling as she watched them play. "For a long time, I didn't think they'd ever learn how to occupy themselves."

"It's amazing how much they've grown and changed over the past ten months," Fallon agreed. "And speaking of changes…have you and Hudson set a date for the wedding?"

"We have," her friend happily confirmed. "Saturday, June 10. We're having the ceremony at the church followed by a reception at Maverick Manor."

"Have you found a dress?"

"I've been looking at bridal magazines and browsing online, but that's it so far. I'm hoping to get to Mimi's Bridal in Kalispell on Saturday, but I have to make sure my maid of honor can go with me."

"Who are you having stand up with you?" Fallon asked.

"Hopefully my best friend," Bella said.

"Me?"

The bride-to-be smiled. "Of course you, if you're willing."

"I would be honored," Fallon told her sincerely.

"And are you up for wedding dress shopping on Saturday?"

"Absolutely. Have you decided who will be your bridesmaids?"

Bella shook her head. "I'm not having any other attendants."

"Why not?" Fallon wondered.

"Because I always imagined that I'd have Dana and Liza in my wedding party," the bride-to-be admitted softly, referring to the two sisters she hadn't seen in years. "And if they can't be there... I don't want anyone else."

Fallon reached over to squeeze her friend's hand in a silent gesture of comfort and support.

"So the wedding party is going to be very small," Bella continued. "Bride and groom, maid of honor and best man, flower girl and two ring bearers."

"Katie, Henry and Jared?" she guessed.

Her friend nodded. "Jamie thinks I'm crazy, but I want my niece and nephews in my wedding party."

"That's not crazy," Fallon assured her. "Crazy would be letting Homer Gilmore anywhere near the wedding punch."

Bella chuckled at her mention of the old man who had confessed to spiking the wedding punch with his homemade moonshine when Jennifer MacCallum and Braden Traub got married last Fourth of July. As a result, the celebration had resulted in several new romances and started the local baby boom. "Apparently he learned his lesson. Although I have to admit, I've found myself wondering if 'what happened at the wedding' wasn't much ado about nothing."

"I'm sure Will Clifton and Jordyn Cates, Lani Dalton and Russ Campbell, Trey Strickland and Kayla Dalton would argue otherwise."

"Hmm."

"I know that tone," Fallon said, sounding a little worried. "What are you thinking?"

"I was just thinking, if Homer Gilmore's moonshine really does have special powers, I should try to get my hands on some."

"Why do you want Homer's moonshine when all of your dreams are about to come true?"

"It wouldn't be for me, but for Jamie."

"I think your brother's hands are full enough with Henry, Jared and Katie," she said.

"I don't mean for him to have more babies," Bella said. "Although there was a definite rise in pregnancies for wedding guests who drank the spiked punch, there was also a noticeable increase in the number of couples falling in love," she pointed out. "That's what I want for Jamie—for him to fall in love, and for real this time."

Fallon didn't say anything. She wasn't going to ask, but her curiosity must have shown on her face because Bella's lips curved into a slow smile.

"Apparently Jamie doesn't tell you *every*thing," his sister mused.

"Maybe that's because he wants to keep his private life private," she suggested. Because she knew that Jamie and Paula's marriage hadn't been without its share of problems, but she also knew that Jamie had loved his wife.

Bella waved a hand dismissively. "If I've learned nothing else this past year, I've learned that keeping secrets doesn't help anyone. My brother needs a wife, his babies need a mother and most of the women in town are keeping a respectable distance because they think he's still mourning Paula.

"I'm not saying he didn't care for her," his sister hastened to explain. "He wouldn't have married her if he didn't believe he was in love with her. But even I could see that they were ill-suited. Paula might have wanted Jamie, but she never really wanted to live in Rust Creek Falls and…" she paused now, as if reluctant to say aloud what she was thinking "… I don't believe she ever wanted those beautiful babies.

"Of course, by the time my brother realized the truth about who she was and what she wanted, they were already married. And Jamie being Jamie, he was determined to make it work."

"She would have loved Henry, Jared and Katie," Fallon said. "If she'd been given a chance to be a mother to them, she would have loved them." Unfortunately, complications resulting from her pregnancy had taken that chance along with her life.

"You always did have a huge and forgiving heart," Bella told her. "And that's what I want for my brother—for him to find someone like you who will help him open his heart again."

She felt her own heart beat faster as she wondered if her friend had somehow guessed the truth of her feelings for Jamie.

But Bella continued, oblivious to Fallon's inner thoughts and deepest emotions. "Someone down to earth, preferably a Rust Creek Falls resident who understands life on a ranch and might be willing to become an instant mother to these precious babies." She grabbed a tissue from the box on the table to wipe the drool off Henry's chin. "Can you think of anyone who might fit the criteria?"

Me! Me! Fallon wanted to respond, while jumping up and down with her hand in the air like an eager second grader.

"I'm sure there are more than a few suitable candidates," she said instead, and hoped her friend didn't guess that her lack of enthusiasm was based on a reluctance to watch Jamie hook up with anyone else.

It had been difficult enough for her to see him with Paula, but she'd tried to be happy for him because she knew he was in love with his wife. She'd been sincerely pleased when he told her about his wife's pregnancy, because she knew how much he wanted to be a father, to have a family of his own. Her heart had ached, but she'd put a smile on her face because she loved him so much she valued his happiness above even her own.

But now, she wasn't sure she could go through that again. She didn't want to sit back and be a spectator while the man she loved fell in love with another woman.

"Has he indicated any interest in meeting someone new?" she asked cautiously.

"No," Bella admitted. "But why wouldn't he be content with the status quo when he's got someone here taking care of his babies every day and often putting a meal on the table? The only thing he's not getting is sex."

Fallon felt her cheeks flush. "How do you know he's not having sex?"

"Because he's too exhausted to ever leave the ranch and find a willing woman," his sister said matter-of-factly.

Which didn't preclude him finding a willing woman *on* the ranch, and that wasn't completely outside the realm of possibility considering that several of the baby chain volunteers were single women. On the other hand, it wasn't very likely with Jamie's sister living under the same roof.

"So what do you think?" Bella prompted. "Can you help me come up with some prospects for him?"

"Sure," Fallon agreed, because apparently she *was* enough of a masochist to play matchmaker for the man she'd been crushing on for more than a decade. Or maybe she was finally ready to face the truth and acknowledge that, if Jamie was ever going to show any interest in her, he would have done so years earlier. But aside from one single, solitary kiss the summer between his first and second years of college, their relationship had never been anything but platonic.

Henry crawled into Fallon's lap, stuffed his thumb in his mouth and dropped his head against her breast. "I think someone's trying to tell me that he's tired."

"Already?" Bella glanced at her watch. "I guess we've been gabbing longer than I realized."

Fallon nodded toward Jared, who had fallen asleep with his cheek on the carpet and a car in his hand. Only Katie was still upright, although Fallon could tell by the little girl's flagging movements that she wouldn't object to being put down for a nap.

Bella helped her get the babies changed and settled into their individual cribs before she headed off to work with a reminder to Fallon about their upcoming trip to the bridal salon.

She was genuinely happy for her best friend, and maybe feeling just a little sorry for herself, because she had no imminent plans for a wedding or a family of her own. But she would put a smile on her face, stand up beside the bride, continue to lavish Henry, Jared and Katie with attention and affection and, most important, pretend that she wasn't seriously infatuated with their father.

Jamie had more than enough work to keep him busy throughout the morning and most of the afternoon. After he checked on the mare and fed the heifers, he worked on fixing the fence on the north border that was in desperate need of repair. Though he couldn't say for certain, the look of the damage—combined with some talk he'd heard in town about Craig Garrison needing parts to fix his ATV—suggested to Jamie that his neighbor's idiot son had run into the fence while he was out joyriding, probably in the middle of the snowstorm a couple of weeks earlier.

He immediately felt guilty for the thought. Craig wasn't really an idiot; he was just a teenager. The spoiled youngest son of a successful rancher who didn't care that Jamie was struggling to keep on top of countless daily tasks without additional fence repairs added to the mix.

He'd bought the Circle K ranch from the bank when Dierk and Gretchen Krueger opted to walk away after the floods decimated their land three years earlier. They'd worked the ranch for almost forty years with the intention of passing it on to their own children someday. But none of their children was interested in the property—especially not after the floods—so they'd opted to sell and move to a more temperate climate for their golden years.

Jamie had been fresh out of school and eager to put down his own roots in Rust Creek Falls independent of the grandparents who had let him and Bella live with them in town but never showed them an ounce of affection. He was also familiar with the Circle K because he'd worked as a ranch hand for Dierk in the summers during high school. The old man had taught him a lot about ranch management, and though Jamie had felt uncomfortable taking advantage of his misfortune, Dierk assured him that he'd be happy knowing the ranch was in the hands of someone who cared about the land and wouldn't turn it into some kind of tourist attraction for the Hollywood types who had been flocking to Montana in recent years to pretend to be cowboys.

So Jamie had scraped together enough money for the down payment, financed the rest of the purchase and taken what was left of the Kruegers' herd on a consignment basis. He renamed the property The Short Hills Ranch in recognition of its topography, then he'd refurbished the house and moved in with his new bride.

He'd been happy then—and so full of hope for the future. Now he was just trying to get by, one day at a time.

That was the problem with physical work—it left his mind free to wander without direction. Usually he appreciated the mundane tasks that he could perform without thinking, but today, Fallon's desire to cut down a tree suddenly had him thinking of Christmases past.

He had fond memories of holidays with his family during the first fifteen years of his life, before his parents had been killed in a car wreck. Hiking out into the woods to find the perfect tree, arguing over who got to cut it down—and then who had to lug it back to the house.

While his father set up the tree, his mother would make hot chocolate, rich and creamy, and float little marshmallows on top. When the chocolate had been drunk, they'd work together to decorate the towering evergreen. Lights. Garland. Ornaments. And then, finally, the serious countdown toward Christmas would begin.

With seven kids in the family, there was always a pile of presents under the tree. Never anything too expensive or impractical, of course, but there was always something that was needed—like an extra pair of long johns or a new razor—and something that was wanted—a coveted toy or favorite treat. And his mother always knitted a new sweater for each of her seven children.

The first Christmas after his parents were gone had been starkly different for Jamie and all of his siblings. Agnes and Matthew Baldwin—their maternal grandparents—were their only living relatives, and they had not been pleased by the prospect of taking in seven grandchildren.

Luke, Daniel and Bailey made it easy on them—opting to leave Rust Creek Falls to make their own way in the world. Because the three eldest siblings were all of legal age, their grandparents couldn't stop them. But Jamie knew that they didn't even try, that they were relieved by this immediate lessening of their responsibilities.

And still, four kids were a lot for the older couple to take in, especially when they lived in a modestly sized house in the center of town. Without any consultation—or even any warning, Agnes and Matthew had signed the two youngest siblings over to the local child welfare authorities to be adopted. Jamie remembered saying goodbye to Dana and Liza before he left for school early one morning, and when he returned home that afternoon, they were gone.

Only Jamie and Bella—too young to be independent like their brothers and too old to be considered adoptable like their sisters—were left. Was it any wonder that he and Bella had adopted a "you and me against the world" mentality? Or that they'd never felt close to the grandparents who had reluctantly taken them in?

Their first holiday with the grandparents had been an eye-opener. Agnes and Matthew hadn't bothered with a real tree for years and didn't see any reason to change their tradition of putting out a ceramic tree on the coffee table. There were a few other decorations scattered around the house and a holly wreath on the exterior door.

He'd thought that was quite possibly the worst Christmas ever. He'd been wrong.

He scrubbed a gloved hand over his face as the cold wind swirled around him, making his eyes water, and forced his attention back to the fence.

A sound came from somewhere in the distance—something that sounded like a dog barking.

He didn't have a dog. He'd always planned to get one, but when he'd suggested to Paula that they make a trip to the nearest shelter to pick one out, she'd balked. If they were going to bring an animal into the house, she didn't want it to be what she called a flea-infested mongrel. And maybe that should have been one of his first clues that their differences were greater than their similarities, but he'd ignored the concerns, so certain that they could make their marriage work.

He heard the bark again—far in the distance. Near the end of the summer, he'd noticed a dog skirting the edges of the property. A once-beautiful golden retriever now with matted fur and distrustful eyes. He didn't know if she'd been abused or abandoned, but she hadn't let him coax her to come near. After a few weeks, he noticed that she hadn't ventured too far away, either.

So he'd put a couple of stainless-steel bowls outside of the barn, ensuring one was always filled with fresh water and the other with kibble he'd picked up when he was at the feed store. And he'd hammered together some spare boards into a makeshift shelter that he'd set out on the north side of the property, where she seemed to linger.

Though he'd never seen her inside, he felt better knowing that it was there, that she had an escape from the elements if she chose to use it. And though he'd never seen her at the barn, the water and food needed to be replenished on a regular basis.

He'd immediately thought of her as a she, though he didn't know for sure. But any uncertainty as to her gender had been put to rest early in October when he'd seen her hovering at the edge of the woods. She was pregnant.

So before the first snowfall, he'd tossed a couple of old blankets into the shelter he'd built, hoping she would take refuge there when her birthing time was near. He wished he could do more. He wished he had the time to track her down and bring her in out of the cold to ensure that she and her puppies were safe, but he had all he could handle taking care of his own kids—and then some.

And now Fallon had launched a Christmas campaign to get him in the spirit of the holidays. He appreciated that her heart was in the right place—he just wished he could make her understand that his was still battered and bruised. He did want HJK's first Christmas to be a memorable one, and he was confident that Fallon would make it so. He was less certain that anything could change his own "bah, humbug" attitude this year, though he was almost tempted to let her try.

Fallon had just finished programming the slow cooker when she heard one of the babies stirring. Wiping her hands on a towel, she quickly climbed the steps to the upper level, eager to get to whoever was awake before he or she woke the others.

She'd been part of the baby chain since the beginning and she'd fallen in love with Henry, Jared and Katie almost instantly. She loved taking care of them and, on the rare days that she didn't see them—and their dad—she missed them all unbearably. On days like today, while she was tending to the children, tidying the house and preparing meals while Jamie worked on the ranch, it was all too easy to pretend that this was her life—that Jamie was her husband and his children were her children, too. But that was only a fantasy. The reality was that when he came in from his chores at the end of the day, she would say goodbye and go back to her regularly-scheduled, lonely life. But today, the fantasy would be extended just a little bit longer, because when Jamie came back, they were going to cut down a Christmas tree together.

After caring for HJK for so long, she'd learned to distinguish the identity of the crier and the nature of their cries. This time it was Henry, she guessed. Either he was hungry, had a wet diaper or a tummy ache. She'd been pleased when he'd crawled into her lap earlier—and a little surprised, because he wasn't usually a cuddler, except when he was tired or sick. She'd assumed he was just tired, but now she wondered.

"How are you doing, big guy?"

He held his arms out to her, a silent plea to be picked up. And though his big blue eyes were swimming with tears, he smiled at her. A quick glance into the other two cribs confirmed that his brother and sister were both sleeping peacefully.

"You didn't nap for very long," she said, speaking

softly as she lifted him into her arms. She patted his bottom, checking his diaper. Though it didn't feel wet, she changed him anyway, then lifted him into her arms again. "You shouldn't be hungry," she said. "Auntie Bella said you had some fruit and eggs this morning, plus a piece of blueberry muffin and a bottle."

"Ba," he said, which was his word for 'bottle.'

"Are you thirsty?" She continued to chat quietly with him as she carried him out of the room and down the stairs. "Or hungry?"

She set him in his high chair and found some grapes in the refrigerator, already washed and cut up so they wouldn't be a choking hazard. She put a few pieces on his tray. He squished them between his fingers then smeared the broken fruit over his tray.

"Okay, not hungry," she decided, as she prepared a bottle for him.

Bella had created charts so that, at the end of the day, Jamie could clearly see each baby's input—the amount of food and drink—and output—the number of wet and dirty diapers. There was also a column for other notes. In the past few weeks, there had been a lot of other notes—explanations for red marks and warnings of possible bruises that attested to their increased mobility.

As Henry continued to muck around with the grapes, Fallon added a tally to the diaper column. Then she wiped off his hands and lifted him out of his high chair again and carried him to the living room.

Although all of the babies could hold their own bottles now, she'd read somewhere that human contact was important for a baby's development—and especially for preemies—and she liked to cuddle with each of them as much as possible. Since Jared and Katie were still sleeping, she took advantage of this one-on-one time with Henry, settling into the rocking chair and offering him the bottle.

He grabbed it with both hands and guided the nipple unerringly into his mouth and immediately began sucking.

"I guess you were thirsty," she noted.

As he continued to drink, she touched her lips to his forehead. Hmm…maybe he was a little warm. And in the late morning sunlight streaming through the window, his cheeks did appear a little blotchy and red.

"Maybe you're cutting some more teeth," she suggested. His bottom central incisors had broken through the gums only a few days earlier—two days later than Katie had cut hers, while his brother, Jared, was still waiting for his.

Henry continued to suck on the empty bottle until she gently eased it from his grasp and set it aside.

"Do you feel better now?" she asked him.

He responded by projectile-vomiting all over her.

Chapter Three

Fallon was having second thoughts about the tree-cutting plan before Jamie came back to the house that afternoon. She'd barely finished cleaning up Henry and herself—having to borrow a shirt from her friend's closet in order to put her own in the wash—when Jared and Katie woke up and began demanding their lunch. Of course, Henry's belly was empty, too, and though she was wary of what might happen with anything he ate, she couldn't let him go hungry.

Thankfully, whatever had upset Henry's tummy earlier seemed to be out of his system, and he dug into his pasta with enthusiasm. After they'd finished eating and she'd finished cleaning up the kitchen, she bundled them into their snowsuits and took them outside to play in the snow. It was fun to watch them crawl around in it, and as an added bonus, it tired them out quickly.

While they were outside, she scanned the property, looking for any sign of their father, but she didn't see Jamie anywhere. She knew he'd planned to fix the fence on the north border of the property, but unless the damage was worse than he'd suggested, he should have been finished by now.

When the babies finally collapsed in the snow, exhausted, she carted them back inside, wrestled them out of their snowsuits, changed their diapers, gave them their bottles and settled them back in their cribs. She touched the back of her hand to Henry's forehead, but whatever had ailed the little guy earlier seemed to have truly passed.

When they were finally all settled, she said a silent prayer of thanks that she was able to get them all to sleep at the same time. By that point, she was just as exhausted as they were.

But she threw another load of laundry into the washing machine, added a couple of items to Jamie's grocery list, and tidied up the toys in the living room because she knew if she sat down, she might not get up again.

She was accustomed to taking care of children all day long. When she wasn't helping with Jamie's babies, she worked part-time at Country Kids Day Care. But she worked with the preschool group, children who generally listened to instruction, sat happily at a table to complete an assigned task and enjoyed story time.

As much as she loved Henry, Jared and Katie—and she did—it wasn't easy trying to keep up with their demands. Although she couldn't deny that they were much easier to deal with now that their schedules were somewhat synchronized. For the first few months, it seemed as if one baby would go down for a nap, then the second would want to be fed, the third would need to be changed and by the time the second one was almost asleep, the first was waking up again.

In those early months, only a few hours with the babies had exhausted her. Thankfully, during that time, there had been a lot of volunteers in the baby chain so that no one had to do more than a four-hour shift and often there were two volunteers during a given period.

Over the past couple of weeks, however, as holiday preparations put more demands on everyone's time, the number of volunteers had started to dwindle. While Fallon understood that people had other responsibilities and obligations, she couldn't abandon Henry, Jared and Katie. Their father was already doing everything he could to keep the ranch running and there was no way he'd be able to do that if he was also responsible for the full-time care of his babies.

The dryer buzzed, signaling the end of the cycle and prompting her return to the laundry room. She knew Jamie appreciated the extra chores she did around the house, but as she folded diapers shirts and sleepers, she found herself wishing that he would—just once—see her as more than a link in the baby chain.

It wasn't quite three o'clock when Jamie returned to the house. After kicking off his boots at the back door, he was immediately struck by the unfamiliar sound of silence. Obviously HJK were down for their afternoon nap—but where was their babysitter?

"Fallon?" he called out.

There was no response. But he did hear water running and realized the sound was coming from the laundry room. As he headed in that direction, he was once again struck by the uncomfortable realization that he would never be able to repay her for everything she'd done for his family over the past ten months—and continued to do. Not only did she take care of his babies, but she also helped prepare meals, kept the house tidy and ensured that HJK—and he—always had clean clothes to wear.

But he could at least thank her, and with that thought in mind, he pushed open the partially closed door to reveal Fallon standing in front of the dryer, shaking out a garment that she'd just removed from it.

He didn't know what it was; he didn't note the shape or color or anything because he couldn't tear his gaze away from Fallon's naked body.

Okay, she wasn't actually naked.

Not even half-naked really.

She was only topless. And wearing a bra. But it had been a long time since he'd seen so much bare female skin. Temptingly smooth and pale. He wondered if it could possibly be as soft as it looked and, from out of nowhere, he was almost overcome by the urge to step forward and press his lips to her bare shoulder.

She turned slightly as she slid an arm into a sleeve, and he realized the garment was a shirt. And now he had an even better view of the bra she was wearing. A barely there scrap of lace with low-cut cups that hugged the curve of her breasts.

He swallowed. Hard.

He started to back away, so that she wouldn't know he'd caught her half-undressed. But he suddenly seemed to be having trouble with blood flow to his brain. Or maybe it was to his legs, because instead of backing out the doorway, he backed into the door, causing it to crash against the wall.

Fallon gasped and whirled around.

Now he had a perfect and unobstructed view of her front, and it was even more spectacular than her back. Because, of course, there were breasts front and center. Delicate swells of creamy flesh that were beautifully showcased by the white lace.

"Jamie!"

He lifted his gaze to her face, saw that her cheeks had turned the same color as her hair. "What?"

"Get out!"

"Oh. Right."

He backed into the door again, then turned around and fled.

Fallon's fingers were unsteady as she worked to fasten the buttons of her shirt. She could still feel the heat in her cheeks, though she didn't think the rush of blood to her face had been the result of embarrassment as much as arousal.

And it had been arousal she'd seen in Jamie's eyes, too. She was certain of it. Okay—*almost* certain.

But how would she know? When had a man ever looked at her with desire in his eyes? Maybe she was just seeing what she wanted to see, because she so desperately wanted to believe he might feel even a tiny bit of what she felt for him.

Aside from some flirting and a few kisses, she didn't have a lot of experience with the opposite sex. Yeah, she'd been hit on occasionally. Probably because there were a lot more men than women in Rust Creek Falls and any woman who walked through the doors of the

Ace in the Hole on a Friday or Saturday night could expect to be hit on. But now that she was thinking about it, she couldn't remember the last time that had happened. True, she hadn't been to the local bar in several months, but since the flood a couple of years earlier, there had been an influx of people from Thunder Canyon and other neighboring towns to help the residents of Rust Creek Falls. And while the majority of those people had gone back to their own homes, many had chosen to stay—most of them women. As a result, the local demographic had shifted. Now that there were a lot more young and single women in town, the local cowboys were happy to spread their attention and affection around.

Fallon had absolutely no objections. She'd never wanted anyone but Jamie. Unfortunately, except for that one kiss seven years earlier, he'd never given her any indication that he felt the same way.

She huffed out a breath and pressed her hands to her still-hot cheeks. Obviously she needed another minute or two before she could face him again. Thankfully, there was the rest of the load of laundry to be folded, which she did while trying not to think about what he'd been thinking when he'd looked at her.

Because it was possible that his wide-eyed, slack-jawed expression had been shock rather than arousal. Certainly he would have been shocked to discover her in his laundry room in a state of semiundress. Maybe even appalled—and wasn't that possibility like a bucket of icy water in her flushed face?

Before she'd finished folding the clothes, she heard, through the baby monitor that she carried with her everywhere she went, sounds of rustling and cooing that were the general precursors to any or all of the triplets waking up. And then she heard Jamie—the low, soothing murmur of his voice as he entered the room and began talking to his children.

She knew it wasn't easy for him—being both a father and a mother to three babies in addition to performing the majority of day-to-day chores that came with owning and managing a ranch. And yet, when he finally got back to the house at the end of his long days, his first thought was always of his children.

Of course, she knew how much family meant to Jamie, and she understood why it was so important to him to ensure that his children always knew how much they were loved. Because he'd been orphaned at fifteen and separated from his siblings soon after. And as far as she knew, neither Jamie nor Bella had heard a single word from any of the others since.

Losing most of his family in such a short period of time had made him determined to keep his own family together, no matter what. Which was why Jamie had been not just furious but deeply hurt when he ran into his grandfather at Crawford's a few months after the babies were born and Matthew Baldwin had suggested that the children might be better off if Jamie put them up for adoption, so they could go to homes with two parents to care for them.

Although Fallon believed the old man had offered this advice out of a sincere desire to help guide his grandson through a difficult situation, she didn't believe it was the right advice. And it renewed her determination to help in any way that she could to ensure that Jamie never needed to worry about losing his children.

When the laundry was folded, she headed upstairs

and found him in the babies' room, changing Katie's diaper. Henry was standing up, holding on to the bars of his crib and chewing on the top rail. Jared was still sleeping, his arms flung out at his sides. He was the only one of the babies who had hated being swaddled as an infant.

"Need a hand?" she asked.

He lifted Katie off of the changing table. "Sure—you can take her downstairs. I'll bring Henry and Jared when they're ready."

"Okay." She took the little girl from his arms, and he immediately turned toward Henry's crib without looking at her.

"Apparently this is going to be awkward," she said, standing beside the changing table with Katie propped on her hip.

"I'm sorry." He carried Henry to the table and began unfastening his overalls.

"Sorry this is awkward?"

He finally lifted his gaze to meet hers. "Sorry I walked in on you in the laundry room," he clarified.

"Forget it," she said. "It was just unfortunate timing."

One side of his mouth curved. "Or fortunate—depending on your perspective."

She felt heat rise into her face again.

"But I wouldn't have walked into the laundry room if I'd known you were in there. Naked," he said.

Her gaze shifted to the trio of cribs lined up along the far wall, settling on the closest one, in which Jared was still sleeping. Of course, none of the babies was paying any attention to their conversation. And even if they had been listening, they wouldn't have understood what the adults were saying. But that knowledge didn't prevent Fallon's cheeks from burning. "I wasn't naked."

"Close enough," he said.

"I was topless," she clarified. "And wearing a bra."

"White lace," he said, confirming that he'd noticed.

"A lot of women wear bathing suits that cover less," she pointed out.

He finished with Henry's diaper and turned back to face her. "Not in Montana in December."

"I'm just saying—it's not a big deal."

"It is to a man who hasn't seen an even partially naked female body in almost fifteen months."

Fifteen months?

He nodded, obviously having read the confusion on her face. "Yeah, the minute Paula found out she was carrying triplets, she shut me out of the bedroom."

Fallon didn't know how to respond to that, so she said nothing.

"So if I was staring—" He shook his head as he set Henry back in his crib so that he could perform the diaper routine with Jared, who was just waking up. "There's no 'if' about it—I was staring. And I'm sorry."

"It's okay," she said, and managed a small smile. "Truthfully, I'm flattered. My breasts are too small to garner much notice."

"Your breasts aren't too small, they're—" He broke off again, swallowed. "Wow, this is a really inappropriate conversation."

"Forget it," she said again. "Please."

"I don't know if I can," he admitted. "But I'll try."

The scent of something rich and savory teased Jamie's nostrils and made his mouth water as he made his way back down the stairs. After setting Henry and Jared in the enclosed play yard with their sister, he headed toward the kitchen, where he could hear Fallon moving around.

"Something smells good," he noted. And looks even better, he thought, surreptitiously glancing at her. Though she was fully dressed now, it was as if he could see right through her clothes to the creamy skin beneath, the tantalizing feminine curves, the peaked nipples pressing against white lace.

"I figured you would probably be ready for dinner by the time we got back from getting the tree," Fallon said, "so I put a roast and vegetables in the slow cooker."

He snapped a leash on his wayward libido and turned his attention to the pot. "We're not eating until we get back?"

"The plan was to go out before it gets dark," she reminded him. "And the roast won't be ready for another hour, anyway. But to be honest, I'm not sure we should get the tree today."

"Why not?" He had no objection to the reprieve, but he was curious as to why Fallon—who had been so eager to get the house decked out for the holidays—had suddenly changed her mind.

Was it his fault? Had his gawking at her nearly naked breasts made her uncomfortable? He mentally shook his head at the ridiculousness of the question. Of course, his gawking had made her uncomfortable. Unfortunately there was no way for him to unsee what he'd seen, even if he wanted to…and he wasn't certain that he did.

"Well, the reason I was doing laundry today—" she glanced away, her cheeks flushing prettily "—is that Henry threw up on me earlier."

"I'm sorry."

"It wasn't your fault," she assured him.

"But I knew he was feeling off," Jamie said, relieved that she didn't blame him for the incident, and especially that she didn't seem to feel uncomfortable after the laundry room encounter. "He was awake a couple of times in the night, not for any particular reason that I could tell, but he was definitely unsettled."

"Well, he seems fine now," she said. "But I'm not sure that being out in the cold for an extended period of time is a good idea."

"My mom always sent us out to play in the winter so the cold could kill off our germs."

The words were out of his mouth before he even knew what he was saying. If she realized the significance of his statement, the implication that she was as close to a mother-figure as his babies had, she didn't show it. In fact, she didn't react at all, except to ask, "What if it wasn't some kind of bug?"

"What else could it be?" he asked.

"Maybe…the muffins I made," she suggested tentatively.

Jamie shook his head. "Your baking did not make him sick."

"How do you know?" she challenged.

"Because all of the babies had the same thing and only Henry threw up."

"So far," she muttered.

"Besides, I ate four of those muffins," he pointed out. "And they were delicious."

She still looked dubious.

"He's fine, Fallon. If I've learned nothing else over the past ten months, I've learned that kids get sick—

and preemies more often than most. There's no way to prevent it," he assured her.

"I've also learned that three babies living in close proximity usually share germs and viruses much more willingly than toys—so it's quite possible that whatever caused Henry's stomach upset might already have been passed on to Jared and Katie."

She nodded in acknowledgment of that fact. "Which is another reason it might be a good idea to delay the tree-cutting."

"That will also give me a chance to haul down the boxes of decorations from the attic," he said. "Because I assume that, after we cut down the tree, you're going to want to decorate it."

"No, *you're* going to decorate it," she said, but softened the directive with a smile.

A smile that drew his attention to her mouth and made him wonder if her lips could possibly be as soft and sweet as they looked. He pushed the tempting question aside. "There you go, being all bossy again," he said, his tone deliberately light.

"But I *might* be persuaded to help," Fallon relented.

He lifted the lid on the pot and peered at the roast beef and vegetables in an effort to avoid focusing on her and the new and unexpected hunger that was churning inside him. "Are you sure it's going to be another hour before it's ready?"

She took the lid from his hand and set it firmly back on top of the stoneware. "Longer if you keep letting all the heat out," she warned.

Except he suspected that her proximity was generating even more heat than the cooking pot. He took a deliberate step away. "Sorry—but I worked through lunch, and dinner smells so good."

She plucked a muffin out of the container on the table and tossed it to him.

He immediately took a bite out of the top, because he was hungry and wanted to reassure her that he had no concerns about the treats she'd baked, but also because focusing on the muffin would help him resist the urge to reach for her. "These are really delicious."

"See? I'm not as incpt in the kitchen as people like to believe."

"Hmm."

She narrowed her gaze. "What's that supposed to mean?"

"Well…that was a pretty awful cake that you took to the potluck." He couldn't resist teasing her a little.

She huffed out a breath and shook her head. "One mistake. *One.* And no one will let me live it down."

"On the other hand, the roast in that Crock-Pot smells really good."

"Crock-Pot cooking is easy," she admitted. "You just toss in the meat and veggies, add some liquid and seasoning, and it pretty much cooks itself."

"Still, I appreciate the effort," he said.

"If that's a 'thank you,' then you're welcome," she said, lifting her coat off the hook by the door.

"Where are you going?" he asked.

"Home."

He should let her go. He needed some time to catch his breath and think about the sudden and unexpected awareness between them—and he couldn't do that while her presence was wreaking havoc on his hormones. But instead of nodding and advising her to 'drive safely,' when he opened his mouth, the only word that came out was, "Stay."

Chapter Four

Fallon raised a brow. "Now who's being bossy?"

But she didn't protest when Jamie took the coat from her hand and returned it to the hook. "You went to the effort of making dinner, you should stay and eat it with us."

"I thought you might appreciate some peace and quiet after a busy day," she said.

"Yeah, me and the triplets—a definite recipe for peace and quiet," he remarked dryly.

Still she hesitated.

"If you don't have other plans, I would enjoy some adult company."

"Bella won't be home for dinner?"

"Not likely," he told her. "She and Hudson are pretty much inseparable these days."

"I guess that makes sense, considering that they're head over heels in love and planning to get married."

His only response was to snag another muffin.

"I thought a dozen of those would last more than a day," she noted, heading back to the living room where the kids were playing.

"I worked up an appetite today," he told her.

She lowered herself to the floor, near the play yard, using the sofa as a backrest. "Did you get the north fence repaired?"

He nodded as he sat down beside her, stretching his legs out in front of him.

She picked up a block that Henry tossed over the enclosure and dropped it back inside for him. "How's Daisy?"

"She seems to be doing okay, if maybe a little restless." He polished off the second muffin as his firstborn continued to play "catch" with Fallon. "How was your day—aside from being vomited on?"

As he'd expected, her cheeks immediately filled with color. "Aside from that, it was good," she said. "Bella asked me to be her maid of honor."

"I thought she would," Jamie said. "You're not just her best friend, you're like a sister to her. To both of us." It was an effort to keep his tone casual, to not reveal any of the inner turmoil he was feeling.

Because while Fallon was like a sister to Bella, she could never take the place of the actual sisters that she'd lost touch with eleven years earlier. And while he wanted to believe she was like a sister to him, their relationship wasn't quite that simple. Especially since he'd seen her half-naked in the laundry room. While he was still trying to get a handle on the feelings churning inside him, he was certain of one thing: those feelings weren't the least bit brotherly.

But maybe he hadn't been as successful at hiding his thoughts as he'd hoped, or maybe Fallon just knew him too well, because she touched his arm. It was simply a gesture of support, but the sight of her hand on his arm made him crave her touch on other parts of his body. He wanted those fingers gliding over his skin, her nails biting into his flesh as he—

Whoa! Not going there. Not with Fallon. No way.

"It's not easy for her, either," she said gently, drawing his attention back to the issue of his sister's wedding. "As excited as Bella is about starting a life with the man she loves, she's going to be thinking of all the people who won't be there on her wedding day."

He nodded. "I'm going to walk her down the aisle, but I'm not giving her away. Aside from it being an archaic tradition, it just doesn't feel right, so we're going to ask the minister to skip that part."

"She'd probably be happy to skip all of the parts that come before 'I now pronounce you husband and wife,'" Fallon said, in what he recognized as a deliberate attempt to lighten the mood.

"Because she knows I wouldn't approve of her moving in with Hudson until he's put the second ring on her finger."

"And you know she wouldn't just abandon you and the babies," she pointed out.

He nodded. "She's already put her life on hold long enough to help us out. And while I sometimes think I should have insisted that she stay at school to get her diploma, there's no way I would have managed this past year without her."

"She'll go back and finish," Fallon assured him.

"Even if she doesn't, she's got Hudson to take care of her now."

Fallon shook her head despairingly. "It's not his responsibility to take care of her," she chided. "When a man and a woman decide to join their lives together, they take care of each other."

She was right, of course. If he let himself think about his parents—which he rarely did—he knew that they'd enjoyed a mutually loving and supportive relationship. But his own experience with marriage had been very different.

At first, it hadn't been so bad. Paula had kept up the house and prepared the meals while he'd handled all of the ranch chores. And he was okay with that, because she was a city girl adjusting to life in Rust Creek Falls. But even that tentative arrangement had fallen apart after the two lines had appeared in the little window of the pregnancy test.

And when his wife had learned that she was carrying three babies, it had been the end of any cooperation or even communication between them. There had been no give-and-take with Paula after that—just a whole lot of unhappiness and anger.

Something beeped in the kitchen, and Fallon pushed herself up off the floor. "Are you still hungry?" she asked.

"Does today end with a *y*?" Jamie asked her.

She smiled at that. "Give me ten minutes to finish up the gravy."

He watched her walk out of the room, his gaze focused on the sexy curve of her butt and the gentle sway of her hips. Of course, when he realized what he was doing—ogling his best friend—he was appalled. But that brief glimpse of her mostly bare torso in the laundry room had reminded him of a simple fact that he'd denied for too long: Fallon O'Reilly wasn't a girl anymore.

Yes, she was his loyal friend and a dedicated caregiver to his babies, but she was also an attractive and appealing woman. Very attractive and incredibly appealing. And the acknowledgment of those simple facts made him a little uneasy, because he had no business thinking of her in those terms.

"Fa!" Henry demanded. "Fa-fa!"

Jamie saw that his son had made his way to the other side of the play yard and was looking toward the doorway through which Fallon had disappeared. All of his kids loved Fallon, but he'd recently begun to suspect that Henry had a little bit of a crush on his second-favorite caregiver—"Auntie Bella" being the favorite of all of them, of course, by simple virtue of the fact that she spent the most time with them.

"Fallon's making dinner for us," he told his son. "Are you hungry?"

"Fa-fa!" Henry said again.

"Fa-fa!" Jared echoed.

Jamie sighed. "What about you?" he asked Katie. "Are you going to join in?"

His baby girl looked up at him with big blue eyes. "Da-da!"

And the sweet sound made his lips curve and his heart swell. "That's my girl," he said, lifting her out of the play yard and into his arms.

Jared's little brow furrowed as he looked up at his sister, outside of the enclosure. He rocked the top rail, shaking the wall. "Da-da!"

"You think that's a get-out-of-jail card now, don't you?"

"Da-da!" Jared said again.

"Fa-fa!" Henry continued.

Chuckling, Jamie unlatched the gate so the boys could escape. Though all of the babies were now able to stand while holding on to something and had even begun to cruise around the furniture, none had yet attempted to take any unsupported steps. As he opened the gate, Henry and Jared dropped to their hands and knees and crawled out of the play yard and headed toward the kitchen.

Fallon was spooning the vegetables into a serving bowl when he walked through the doorway with Katie still in his arms. Henry's and Jared's palms slapped against the tile floor as they hurried to keep up with his pace.

"Perfect timing," she said, as she set the bowl on the table beside a platter of meat. The promised gravy had already been poured into a pitcher and there was a basket of warm dinner rolls, too.

Jamie buckled the kids into their high chairs and washed their hands while Fallon finished cutting up their meat and vegetables into bite-sized pieces. As he sat down across from her at the table, he realized that he was glad she was there. He'd invited her to stay because it seemed like the polite thing to do, but he was sincerely pleased that she'd agreed. Not just because he appreciated an extra set of hands to help with HJK, but because it was nice to have someone to talk to at the end of the day. *A friend*, he reminded himself firmly.

For a long time, it had been just him and his sister—and the three babies, of course, but they didn't yet add much to a dinner conversation. He was happy for Bella, that she'd met Hudson and fallen in love. And even if— according to Fallon—it wasn't Hudson's job to take care of Bella, Jamie knew that he would. Just as he knew that Bella would take care of Hudson, too.

If he had any concerns, they weren't about the upcoming nuptials but the practicalities of managing the triplets every day without his sister living under the same roof. He knew that she would continue to help in any way that she could, but he didn't want her to. She needed to focus on her own life, her own future, and her own happiness. The successful management and operation of the baby chain had allowed him to become complacent, but it was time for him to stop dragging his heels and make other arrangements for the care of his children.

But for now, he had different concerns. "So when do you want to get the tree?" he asked, as he sliced into a piece of roast beef. "Saturday?"

Fallon shook her head. "I promised to go wedding dress shopping with Bella on Saturday."

"They just got engaged. I didn't think she'd be rushing into that already," he commented.

"They're planning a June wedding," she reminded him. "And that's only six months away."

"Still, dress shopping won't take all day, will it?"

"A woman's wedding day is one of the most important days of her life," she pointed out to him. "And considering that all of the attention is on the bride and what she's wearing, I'm not going to rush your sister into making a decision."

"Okay, so Saturday's out," he conceded. "How about Sunday?"

"Attendance at my parents' house for Sunday dinner is mandatory, but I could maybe come by in the afternoon," she suggested.

"That sounds good," he agreed. "Plus it gives me a few days to haul the decorations down from the attic."

"You haven't said anything about the other items on my list," she noted.

He speared a chunk of potato with his fork. "Isn't it enough that I'm agreeing to put up a tree?"

Fallon shook her head despairingly as she chewed on a carrot. "Have you started your Christmas shopping yet?"

"Bella's picked up a few things for me to give to the kids."

"What about S-A-N-T-A?"

He lifted his glass to his mouth to hide his smile. "Santa?"

She scowled at him as she jerked her head toward the trio of high chairs, where Henry, Jared and Katie were intently focused on shoving food into their mouths and not paying the least bit of attention to the adults' conversation.

"Maybe you should clarify what you're asking," he suggested.

"I'm asking you who's going to help Saint Nicholas with his shopping," she told him.

"I'll figure it out." He slid another piece of the tender meat between his lips.

Of course, Fallon wasn't satisfied with that vague response. "When?" she pressed.

He shook his head. "You're relentless, aren't you?"

"I know a lot of guys take pride in doing all of their

shopping on Christmas Eve, but you can't do that when you have kids," she told him.

"Maybe not in a few years," he acknowledged. "But right now, they don't even know what Christmas is. Whatever Santa brings, they'll probably be more interested in the boxes than the toys."

Before she could dispute his point, the back door was flung open and Bella stomped in, kicking snow off of her boots. "It's really coming down out there," she said, as she pulled a knit hat off of her head and unfastened her coat.

Fallon turned to look out the window, her eyes widening as she noticed the thick, fluffy flakes illuminated by the porch lights. "When did the snow start?"

"About half an hour ago," Bella said, hanging her coat on an empty hook. Having taken off her boots, she now stuffed her feet inside a pair of fuzzy slippers. "A couple of inches have fallen already and we're supposed to get another eight to ten before morning."

"That's my cue to be heading home," Fallon decided, pushing away from the table.

"Do you want me to give you a lift?" Jamie offered.

She rolled her eyes as she dropped quick kisses on top of each of the babies' heads. "I've been driving in Montana for as long as I've been driving," she reminded him. "I'm not afraid of a little snow."

"Eight to ten inches is more than a little snow," he pointed out.

"Which is why I'm heading out now." She reached for her coat and turned to Bella, "Let me know what time you want to leave Saturday morning."

His sister nodded. "I will."

"And I'll see you guys Sunday," she said to Jamie,

encompassing the triplets with her remark and adding a wave for their benefit.

Henry lifted a hand, covered with the remnants of smushed potato and gravy, and waved back.

"Bu-bu-bu," Katie said, which was one of her favorite sounds and used to mean "bye-bye," "bottle," "ball" and "Bella."

"What's Sunday?" Bella asked, when Fallon had gone.

"We're going to get the Christmas tree on Sunday," Jamie told her.

His sister held a washcloth under the faucet, then wrung it out and wiped the triplets' hands and faces. "I thought you were planning to do that today."

"Plans changed."

Bella cleared away the babies' plates, then filled the kettle with water and set it on the stove to boil. "So what did I miss?"

Jamie mopped up the leftover gravy on his plate with a piece of roll. "Roast beef."

She shook her head. "I wasn't talking about that."

"What were you talking about?"

"I got the impression that I walked into the middle of something."

"Just dinner," he told her.

"Hmm," she said, clearly unconvinced.

"Did you eat?" he asked.

She nodded. "Hudson and I grabbed a bite at the Ace."

He frowned at that. "You know I don't like you hanging out there."

"I wasn't hanging out," she chided. "I was having a

meal in the company of my fiancé on a Thursday night. And you're changing the subject."

"What subject?" he asked.

"Fallon."

He carried his empty plate and cutlery to the dishwasher. "I didn't realize she was a subject."

"Neither did I, but there was a definite vibe between the two of you when I walked in," she told him.

"What kind of vibe?"

"That's what I'm trying to figure out," she admitted.

"Well, while you're doing that, I'm going to get HJK washed up and ready for bed," he said, and made his escape before his sister asked more questions he wasn't prepared to answer.

As he led the babies toward the stairs—because it was a lot easier to let them crawl than attempt to carry all of them—he wondered if she'd actually picked up on some kind of "vibe" between him and Fallon or was just toying with him.

Since Bella had accepted Hudson's proposal, she'd suddenly decided that he needed to find someone to share his life, too. More important, she believed that his children needed a mother. Jamie knew that she didn't mean to be insensitive—that she genuinely wanted what was best for his family. He also suspected that she knew more about the issues behind the scenes in his marriage than he'd ever admitted to her.

But he wasn't looking for anyone to share his life. In fact, as much as he appreciated the baby chain, he sometimes resented the presence of other people in his home and taking care of his children. Which was completely unreasonable, of course, but true nonetheless.

And yet, when he had the opportunity to share a meal

alone with his children, he'd invited Fallon to stay. But Fallon wasn't just a link in the baby chain. She was one of his best friends.

And now he'd seen her half-naked.

He hadn't been joking when he'd told her that he didn't know if he could forget seeing her topless in the laundry room. The tantalizing image seemed to be indelibly imprinted on his memory.

After the triplets were settled into their respective cribs and sleeping soundly, he spent some time in the main floor office paying bills and ordering supplies. He loved being a rancher—he didn't love the financial instability that came with the title. And he didn't love being dependent on other people to take care of his babies while he was busy with the numerous tasks required to keep the ranch running.

He wouldn't have made it through this past year without the baby chain, and especially without his sister. And while putting the triplets into day care would ease his reliance on community help, it wouldn't affect his daily routine very much—if at all. He would still be the one who fed them their dinner—even if the meals would likely be prepared by volunteers—bathe them and put them to bed.

But he knew the whole dynamic in the house would change when Bella married Hudson. And Jamie suspected it might not be too long after that before they'd want to start their own family. His sister deserved to be a mother to her own children, but he knew that her absence would leave an enormous hole in his life and the lives of his children.

Maybe he should think about finding a new mother for his children, but aside from the fact that he had no energy to get dressed up and go out when he finally finished his chores at the end of the day, he had less than zero interest in dating. Even if he had the time, he didn't know that he was willing to put himself out there again.

He'd made a major error in judgment with Paula. On his own for the first time, away from Rust Creek Falls and the rules and responsibilities that had been such an integral part of his life, he'd relished the freedom. And when he'd met Paula, he'd been blinded by her beauty and seduced by her charm.

They'd been together for almost three years and heading toward graduation when he asked her to marry him. They were both young, maybe too young to be thinking about lifetime commitments, but the alternative—going their separate ways—had been unthinkable to him.

His sister hadn't been thrilled when he'd told her about his imminent wedding plans. He'd thought Bella was just feeling out of sorts, or was still mad at him for going away to school and abandoning her in the care of their cold grandparents. Whatever her motivation, she'd warned him that Paula wouldn't enjoy ranch life. In fact, she'd questioned whether the Seattle native would be able to stick it out through a single Montana winter.

He should have listened to his sister. Because although Paula had endured three long and frigid winters, she hadn't been happy in Rust Creek Falls. She didn't like the weather or the isolation or even, by the end, the man she'd married.

If Jamie ever did decide to marry again—or even start dating again—he would choose a local girl. Someone who knew what it meant to live on a ranch, someone who loved the land—and especially someone who loved his children.

Someone like Fallon.

He shook his head, as if that might dislodge the thought from his mind. Fallon O'Reilly might be the perfect woman for him in a lot of ways, but she was also completely wrong for just one reason: she was his best friend. And that was a line he wasn't going to cross. Ever. No matter how much he was tempted by the image of her in white lace.

By the time he finally finished his paperwork, shut down the computer, checked on the kids and crawled beneath the covers of his bed, he was exhausted. Accustomed to the early mornings and long hours of running a ranch, he'd learned to fall asleep quickly even if he didn't sleep as deeply as he used to. He was so attuned to the sounds that his children made, he could often hear them stirring and tell when they were about to waken before they actually did so.

But tonight, his own sleep was elusive. Because every time he closed his eyes, he saw Fallon as she'd looked in the laundry room. Her back—long and narrow, the ridges of her spine visible beneath her creamy skin. The expanse of bare flesh broken only by the narrow band of white lace that stretched across her middle and tiny straps that went over her shoulders. The sweet little indent at the small of her back, just above the waistband of her jeans. The sexy slope of her strong shoulders. He could have stared contentedly at her back for hours—then she'd turned around.

He pressed the heels of his hands to his eyes. He shouldn't be remembering Fallon like this. They'd been friends for a lot of years. She'd been his confidante through some of the darkest periods in his life. She was the only person who knew about some of the worst days of his marriage. The one person he'd always trusted to listen and not judge. The one person who had always been there for him when he needed someone. And it would screw up everything if he let himself want her.

In the past ten months, he hadn't experienced even the most basic stirrings of physical attraction. He'd been too exhausted to feel much of anything. And that was okay. Every free minute he had, he spent with his kids. And every day, he sent up a prayer of thanksgiving that he'd been given the gift of three beautiful, healthy babies. He didn't think about romance except to think that he might be ready to start dating again around the time that HJK were ready to start school—as in college. He hadn't expected to feel any kind of sexual awakening before then—and especially not for his childhood friend.

Okay, so there had been that one kiss, more than seven years earlier. A kiss that never should have happened. A kiss that had, nevertheless, lingered in his mind for a long time afterward. The sweetness of her lips, the softness of her body, the absolute perfection of that one stolen moment.

Maybe he'd briefly considered the possibility of allowing that kiss to lead to something more. But even then, he'd valued her friendship too much to jeopardize that relationship for the sake of a sudden and unexpected attraction. Thankfully, he'd left the next day for his second year at college, grateful for the time and distance to get his head back on straight.

A few weeks later, he'd met Paula, and he'd pushed all non-platonic thoughts about Fallon to the back of his mind.

Neither he nor Fallon had ever mentioned the kiss

again. And when he'd told her that he was getting married, she wasn't anything but supportive. Even after the wedding, she'd continued to be there for him, listening to his hopes and dreams, worries and frustrations.

He'd told her things he'd never told anyone else, because she was firmly and unequivocally in the "friend" camp. Discovering her half-naked in the laundry room had apparently shifted her into the "want to get naked with" camp.

At the very least, he wanted to know if she was wearing white lace panties that matched her bra. And did she prefer bikinis or boy shorts or hi-cut briefs? The formation of the question in his mind proved that he'd spent too much time thumbing through the pages of the Victoria's Secret catalog his sister had left on the kitchen table.

Maybe he wasn't ready to think about getting married again. Maybe he wasn't even ready to start dating again. But his body was definitely in favor of ditching the celibacy phase that had never been his idea. Thankfully, his rational mind knew that thinking about Fallon in conjunction with that plan was a very bad idea.

Unfortunately, his subconscious didn't agree. And when he finally fell asleep, he dreamed about her in his arms…and in his bed.

Chapter Five

Jamie pulled HJK's sleigh over the snow, toward the woods on the west side of his property, while Fallon walked beside him, dragging an empty toboggan onto which he would secure the tree that they cut down. The air was cold and crisp, typical of Montana in December, the snow crunching beneath their feet.

Fallon was wearing slim-fitting jeans tucked into knee-high winter boots, a navy ski jacket with a pink pom-pom hat and matching mittens. The color should have clashed horribly with the red curls that peeked out beneath her cap, but it didn't. Instead, she looked like she'd walked off the front cover of an L.L. Bean catalog—a woman as comfortable in her clothes as she was in her surroundings.

He wondered how it was that he'd known her forever, but every once in a while, he would look at her as if he was seeing her for the first time and be struck by how truly beautiful she was. Today was one of those days. While he viewed this outing as a chore, she was obviously excited about their purpose and it showed in the color in her cheeks and the sparkle in her eyes.

He halted at the edge of the tree line and turned to her. "Okay, pick a tree."

"Me?" she said, obviously surprised.

"Isn't that why we're here?"

"No, we're here because you need a Christmas tree," she reminded him. "I only agreed to tag along because I knew there was no way you could chop down a tree and get it—along with three babies—back to the house on your own."

"No, you're here because you didn't trust that I'd comply with your list," he guessed.

"That, too," she confirmed, not even attempting to hide her smile. "But this is really about sharing—or starting—family traditions with your children."

"If you expected three ten-month-old babies would have any input in selecting a tree, you're going to be disappointed."

"Why would you say that?"

He gestured to the sleigh, where Henry, Jared and Katie had all fallen asleep.

Fallon sighed. "I should have remembered that the motion of the sled knocks them out."

"Looks like it's up to you and me," Jamie said.

She didn't let herself read too much into his words. Didn't want to admit—even to herself—how much she wished there was a "you and me" that included her and Jamie.

"It's your tree," she reminded him. "So you should pick."

"Okay. How about that one?"

Of course, he was pointing to the closest one for, she suspected, no reason except that it was the closest one. She looked the tree up and down, then walked around it, emerging again from the other side shaking her head. "It's too big."

He pointed to another undoubtedly random tree. "That one?"

She immediately nixed that suggestion, too. "That one's too small."

"Make up your mind, Goldilocks."

"Goldilocks?"

He reached out and tugged on the end of one of her curls. "Your hair might be the wrong color," he acknowledged. "But you've mastered the picky part."

"There's a difference between being picky and discerning," she told him. "And this shouldn't be an impulsive decision. You have to think about where you're going to put the tree, you should check to ensure there aren't any big gaps between the branches, that the trunk is relatively straight and the needles are healthy."

He swept his arm out, gesturing to the wooded area. "Pick a tree—please."

She performed a quick visual scan of the area, then did another walk around a different tree. "This one," she decided.

He glanced from the one she'd selected to his original choice and back again. "That's the same size as the first one I picked."

"The same height," she allowed. "But it's not as full, so it won't take up as much space in the living room."

Though he still looked skeptical, he shrugged. "Okay."

He picked up the saw and moved closer to the tree. Before he started cutting, though, he reached between the branches to grab hold of the trunk and give the tree a good shake to dislodge any critters that were making it their home.

The branches were pretty low to the ground, so Jamie cut off the lowest ones before he crouched down to attack the trunk.

Fallon stood out of the way, keeping an eye on the still-sleeping babies, while Jamie got started. Though she would never admit it to him, she enjoyed watching him work—especially in the hot summer months when he'd strip down to his jeans and T-shirt. Well-worn jeans that molded to the strong muscles of his butt and thighs, and simple T-shirts that stretched over his broad shoulders.

Today, in deference to the frigid winter weather, he was wearing a sheepskin-lined leather jacket over a flannel shirt over one of those T-shirts. Despite the layers, she couldn't help appreciating the width of those shoulders, the obvious strength in his arms. He was incredibly and beautifully built, with the kind of rock-hard muscles that were honed through years of ranch life and could never be replicated in a gym.

It always made her heart sigh to see this strong man being so gentle with his babies. To watch those big hands fasten the tiny snaps on a diaper shirt or affix a miniature barrette in Katie's wispy hair. And whenever she caught him snuggling one of those tiny babies against his broad chest…well, if she'd been the type to swoon, that scene would have made her do so.

Thankfully, he seemed oblivious to the effect he had on her. Not just because of their long-time friendship but because she knew he was grieving the loss of his wife, and it would take time for his heart to heal. But she also knew that he had an incredible capacity for love, because she saw evidence of it every time he was with his babies. And there was a tiny blossom of hope inside of her heart that maybe, someday, he might love her, too. In the meantime, she was content to be part of his life and shower all of her love on his children.

When the tree was strapped down on the sled, with the saw secured beneath it, they headed back toward the house. Henry, Jared and Katie never woke up. Not until Fallon helped Jamie lift them out of the sled and extricate them from their snowsuits.

After they were settled in their play yard with an assortment of favorite toys, Jamie wrestled the tree into the living room. The pungent scent of fresh pine filled the air and filled Fallon's heart with nostalgia. Christmas truly was her favorite time of the year. She had so many wonderful memories of the holidays with her family, so many traditions they still shared—shopping and wrapping, baking and caroling—and those were what she wanted to help Jamie create with his family.

She understood his reticence. The holidays hadn't been a lot of fun for him in the years following his parents' deaths. And, of course, this was his first Christmas without his wife. But it was also his first Christmas with his babies, and she knew that if he could be convinced to make an effort for them, he would find joy in the celebration, too.

And putting up a Christmas tree was, she believed, a first step in the right direction. Which was why she was on her stomach on the floor in the middle of the room, holding the base while he maneuvered the stump in place.

Thankfully, he'd had the foresight to cut off some more of the lower branches before bringing the tree into the house, so she wasn't completely suffocating beneath it. When it was finally in place, she tightened the screws, then wriggled out from beneath the branches and stood up beside him. "What do you think?"

He tilted his head and considered. "I think it's a little crooked."

"It looks great," she assured him.

"Maybe if I—"

"No."

He frowned. "You don't even know what I was going to say."

"It doesn't matter," she said. "You don't need to do anything. The tree is perfect just the way it is."

"Perfect?" he echoed skeptically.

"Perfect doesn't have to mean without flaws," she told him. "Sometimes it only refers to what fulfills your need in the moment."

He held her gaze for a long moment, and something in the depths of his blue eyes made her suspect that he was thinking of needs unrelated to the upcoming holiday. The intensity of his stare made her heart pound and her blood pulse.

Then his attention shifted to the tree again. "In that case, I'd say this perfect tree doesn't need any lights or decorations."

"And you'd be wrong," she said, pleased that her even tone gave no hint of her inner turmoil.

"I figured you would say that," he admitted.

Fallon opened one of the boxes he'd brought down from the attic, looking for lights. The boxes were clearly labeled, but for some reason the contents didn't match the tags. She finally found the lights in the third box she opened—the one marked "Tree Decorations." She had yet to find the actual tree decorations. As for the lights—

She sighed.

"What's wrong?"

Jamie winced when she held up a tangle of wires and miniature bulbs.

"Oh."

"Who put these away like this?" she asked.

"I guess I did," he admitted.

She tossed him the knotted mess. "Then you can untangle them."

He didn't grumble too much about the assigned task. Of course, she ended up helping, because nothing else could go on the tree until the lights were on.

"How was shopping with my sister yesterday?" he asked, as he picked up a second strand of lights.

Thinking back to the hours she'd spent in Kalispell with Bella made her smile. "It was a lot of fun."

"Did she find a dress?" he wondered.

"She didn't tell you?"

"I've hardly seen her," he admitted. "I heard her come in late last night, then as I came in from the barn this morning, she was on her way out again."

"Yes, she found a dress," she told him, replacing a burned-out bulb while he continued working at the knots. "After trying on about thirty different styles— and looking fabulous in every single one—she finally went back to the first one that had caught her eye. Then she had to choose her veil and shoes and…well, you probably don't want to know what your little sister's going to be wearing under her gown, but I can confidently assure you that she's going to be the most beautiful bride Rust Creek Falls has ever seen."

Too late, Fallon remembered that Jamie and Paula had been married in town, at the same church where Bella and Hudson planned to exchange their vows. And, of course, his wife had been stunning—a veritable fairy-tale princess in an elaborate white gown with a full skirt heavy with crystals and beads. Unfortunately, their marriage had not led to happily-ever-after.

"Or at least the most beautiful bride next June," she amended.

"You don't have to watch what you say around me," Jamie told her. "We've been friends too long for you to worry about censoring your words now."

"I know," she agreed. "But I also know this whole year has been incredibly difficult for you, and it must be hard to feel happy for Bella when your own marriage didn't turn out the way you hoped it would."

"I can't deny that my marriage wasn't what I'd hoped, but it isn't hard to be happy for my sister," he said. "Maybe I am a little concerned that everything seems to be happening so fast, but there's no denying how much Hudson adores her or how happy they are together, and that's all I want for her—to be happy."

"She says the same thing about you," Fallon told him.

"I know," he admitted. "But right now, I'm focusing on being grateful. I've been blessed with three wonderful kids and I feel like it would be selfish to want anything more."

"Wanting to win the lottery might be selfish. Wanting to be happy is human."

"Are you happy?" he asked, looking up from the tangle of wires and meeting her eyes.

She stood up with a strand of lights in her hand. "How did this get to be about me?"

"I know you've always wanted to get married and have kids of your own," he continued, turning his attention back to his task. "But you've put that dream on hold for the better part of ten months to take care of my family."

"Maybe." She climbed onto the step stool he'd set up by the tree. "But I don't regret a single minute of it."

"What are you doing?" he demanded, dropping the lights and crossing the floor in three quick strides until he was standing by the stool.

"What does it look like I'm doing?" she countered.

"It looks like you're trying to kill yourself," he said, lifting his hands to her hips to hold her steady.

Except that she'd been steady—until he touched her. Now she could feel the imprint of his hands through the denim, and her knees felt weak and shaky.

"You're not supposed to stand on the top step," he admonished.

"I can't reach the tree top if I don't," she pointed out.

"Then get down from there and let me do it," he suggested.

"If you want me to get off the stool, you need to move away."

"If I move away, you're going to fall," he countered.

She rolled her eyes as she shifted her feet to turn around. And realized her new position left Jamie looking directly at her crotch. And while he'd loosened his grip enough to let her turn, the lighter touch of his hands on her hips felt almost like a caress. Now her legs started a full-on wobble.

"I, uh, need to get down," she said.

"I've got you," he promised.

If his words were intended to reassure her, they had the opposite effect. She took one step down, then another, but he didn't shift away, which meant that by the time her feet were firmly on the floor, their bodies were so close they were nearly touching.

She tipped her head back to look at him, and found his eyes—those deep blue eyes—were fixed on hers. This his gaze dipped to her mouth, and her breath caught in her lungs.

"Fa-fa!" Henry called, the familiar and impatient demand finally breaking the spell that seemed to have woven around Fallon and Jamie.

She attempted to step back, and stumbled against the stool she'd actually, stupidly, forgotten was there. But Jamie still had his hands on her hips, so she didn't fall. His lips twitched at the corners, as if he was trying not to smile. Not to laugh at her. She felt her cheeks flush—the curse of being a redhead. Embarrassed and annoyed, she shoved the strand of lights at him.

"Fine, you put these on the tree while I finish untangling the rest."

He had to let go of her to catch the lights, and then he finally stepped away from her.

"Fa-fa," Henry chanted again.

She shifted her attention to the baby, who was standing up and holding on to the top of the gate. "What's up, big guy?"

He pointed to the rubber ball he'd thrown to her.

"You want to play catch?"

He grinned, showing her his six tiny white teeth. She scooped up the ball and tossed it back into the enclosure. He let go of the gate to clap his hands together.

Fallon gasped softly. "Jamie!"

"I see him," he said, his voice close behind her.

"He's standing up without holding on to anything."

The words were barely out of her mouth before he wobbled, then fell back onto his butt. His eyes opened wide, as if he wasn't sure what had happened, and then his lower lip began to tremble.

"You're okay," Fallon told him, deliberately employing the sing-song tone of voice that was usually effective in diverting a meltdown. "You were up, and then you went down, that's all."

His lip stopped trembling.

"Up then down," she said again, then clapped her hands together. "Yay!"

He clapped his hands together, too.

Jamie reached over the wall of the enclosure to ruffle his son's hair. "Way to go, big guy."

Henry grinned, obviously proud of himself even if he wasn't sure why.

"Make sure you note the date in his baby book," Fallon said.

"I will," he promised. "I missed the first time he rolled over—actually, the first time each one of them rolled over—so there's no way I'll forget this milestone."

He stepped up onto the bottom step of the stool—because he was at least six inches taller than she was and had longer arms, too—and began winding the lights around the tree.

"Don't just hang them off the ends of the branches," Fallon admonished. "Wrap them around each branch, up one side and back down the other."

"What's wrong with the way I'm doing it?" he wanted to know.

"Aside from the fact that it's sloppy and lazy, you won't have any light emanating from inside the tree."

"You're being picky again," he told her.

"Discerning," she countered.

"And these needles are prickly."

"Just like your attitude."

His lips curved at that. "Fine. I'll do it your way," he relented. "But as soon as I get the highest branches done, I'm letting you take over."

She handed him another strand of lights. "Are you sure you can trust me to stand two feet off the ground?"

"No, but it's unlikely you'd break a leg falling from that height."

She continued to untangle lights while he worked at wrapping the tree, muttering under his breath whenever the needles poked his skin.

"Did you grumble this much when you put the lights on your tree last year—or did Paula do it?"

He snorted. "Paula wasn't exactly in the holiday spirit last year, so I picked up a tree from the lot down by Crawford's."

"I guess, being five months pregnant with triplets, she wasn't up to hiking half a mile through the snow to chop down a blue spruce," she said, wishing she hadn't mentioned his wife's name.

"Or even decorate it," he admitted.

"She didn't tell you what ornaments she wanted where?"

He shook his head. "By December, we were barely on speaking terms."

"I know you went through a rough patch," she said softly. "But I didn't know it was that bad."

"It wasn't something I wanted to talk about, with anyone," he admitted. "And, of course, everyone thinks I've spent the past ten months mourning the loss of my wife, but the truth is, our happy marriage was an illusion. Even if she hadn't died, we wouldn't be celebrating this holiday together."

"What do you mean?"

"She was planning to leave after the babies were born."

Fallon shook her head. "I don't believe it."

"It's true," he told her. "You remember how I told you that she wasn't happy to discover that she was carrying triplets?"

"Sure," she agreed. "But any woman would be daunted by the prospect of birthing and caring for three babies. I imagine you were a little apprehensive yourself."

"More than a little," he admitted. "The difference is that I always wanted a big family—even if I assumed they would come one at a time."

She lifted a hand to his arm, drawing his gaze to her. "She was scared and overwhelmed, but she would have come around," she said softly.

"I'm not so sure," he confided. "Before Christmas last year, she made it clear that the babies would be my responsibility because she was going back to Seattle and filing for divorce."

"I don't believe it," Fallon said again. "I mean, I believe that she said it," she clarified. "But I don't believe she would have done it. She loved you, Jamie."

He appreciated the sentiment, but he no longer believed it was true. Maybe Paula had loved him when she married him, but any affection she'd felt for him in the beginning was long gone before her premature labor. Pushing the unhappy memories aside, he turned his attention back to the lights.

Although he'd threatened to make Fallon do the lower half of the tree, by the time he was halfway, it seemed easier just to finish the task. When the lights were on, she handed him the garland, and he draped that along the branches while she found the boxes of decorative bows and balls and other ornaments.

She chatted to HJK while she was opening boxes and unwrapping ornaments, carrying on a one-sided conversation that kept them engaged while they played. Watching her with his children, Jamie never ceased to be amazed by her natural ease with them. She had an innate ability to anticipate their wants and needs, offering comfort and support while also encouraging them to push their own boundaries and try new things. He had no doubt she'd make a great mother one day.

He hung a red cardinal-shaped ornament on a branch in the middle of the tree and stepped back. "That's the last one."

"Not quite," Fallon said, handing him a medium-sized square box with a red bow on the top.

"What's this?"

"Open it and see."

He lifted the lid to uncover three frosted ornaments nestled in separate compartments. Two of them were adorned with sets of blue footprints on the front and the third with pink footprints. He lifted one from the box and turned it over to see that there was a date and an inscription on the other side: Henry's First Christmas.

The other ornaments were similarly marked with Jared's and Katie's names and the date.

"These are great, Fallon."

"I saw the woman who makes them at a craft show in Kalispell last month and immediately put in my order," she told him. "They look like glass but they aren't. I didn't see any point in a keepsake ornament that would break the first time it fell off a branch."

"I never thought about getting something like this... something to commemorate the occasion," he admitted, moved by her thoughtfulness.

"You would have," she said confidently. "But I saw them first and couldn't resist."

"You give me too much credit."

She shook her head. "You don't give yourself enough. I can only imagine how hard it must be to keep the ranch running and take care of three babies all by yourself."

"I don't do it by myself," he reminded her. "There's no way I could manage without Bella and all the baby chain volunteers...and you."

"You don't have to," she assured him.

He managed a smile at that. "I can't expect the baby chain to operate forever."

"Of course, it won't be forever. In another four years, the triplets will be ready for school."

"Only another four years?"

She bumped her shoulder against his playfully, and the soft curls on top of her head brushed against his jaw. "You're going to make it."

"I appreciate your vote of confidence," he said,

breathing in the scent of her shampoo—strawberries and cream, sweet and tempting.

She glanced at the clock on the mantel and winced. "And if I'm going to make it home in time for family dinner, I need to run."

After a quick check on the babies, he followed her to the door, where she was already zipping up her coat. She tugged her pom-pom hat onto her head again, and he lifted a hand to her hair.

She went completely still. "What are you doing?"

"You've got a pine needle caught in your curls," he told her.

"Oh."

He attempted to work it free—without much success. He was trying to extricate it without pulling her hair, but the curls seemed reluctant to let go of the needle, and he found himself reluctant to remove his fingers from her soft tresses.

"Don't worry about it," she said, after about half a minute had passed with no apparent success. "My hair is—"

"I've got it," he assured her. "Just give me a second."

It probably wasn't much more than that before he lowered his hand from her curls with the long green needle pinched between two fingers.

"Thanks," she said, a little breathlessly.

"Thank *you*," he countered. "I wasn't really looking forward to the tree decorating but you made it fun."

"Only the first of many fun activities on my list," she promised.

Which somehow started him thinking of fun activities that he knew weren't on her list. Activities of a much more personal nature.

He blamed those thoughts for what he did next: he dipped his head toward her, tempted almost beyond reason by the sexy curve of her lips. Tempted to sample her sweetness, to taste and take like a starving man at a banquet until he was finally sated by her flavor.

But at the last moment, he shifted and touched his lips to her cheek instead.

Because kissing her would change everything between them, and he wasn't sure that he was ready for things to change—or if he ever would be.

Chapter Six

"Sorry, I'm late," Fallon said, kissing her mother's cheek as she hurried past her to wash up at the sink.

Maureen O'Reilly glanced up from the potatoes she was mashing. "Where have you been?"

"At The Short Hills Ranch." She turned on the faucet, squirted some soap on her hands and rubbed them together to create a foamy lather.

Her mother punched the masher into the potatoes again. "With Jamie Stockton," she said, her statement of the obvious spoken in a tone of disapproval.

"Yes, with Jamie and the triplets," Fallon clarified, focusing all of her attention on rinsing the soap off of her hands and willing the heat to fade from her cheeks—one of which had recently been brushed by Jamie's lips. "We chopped down and decorated their Christmas tree."

"It's nice that you were there to help," Maureen acknowledged. "But maybe you should let Jamie celebrate those kinds of family traditions with his family."

"His sister spends most of her time with her fiancé, the rest of his siblings are scattered, he barely speaks to his grandfather and his children are more of a hindrance than a help at their age." She grabbed a towel to dry her hands and tried not to think about the kiss—if the brief contact could even be considered a kiss. "Not everyone is fortunate enough to have a family like ours."

The explanation seemed to appease Maureen, at least a little.

"Well, now that you're here, you can finish setting the table. Brenna got it started, but then she got a text from one of her friends who just broke up with her boyfriend and she's been on the phone ever since."

She was happy to be given a task that would allow her to escape the scrutiny of her mother's eagle eye, but had to ask, "Where's Fiona?"

"She ran into town to pick up ice cream for the apple crisp."

"Mmm, I thought I smelled apples baking."

Fallon peeked into the dining room to see how much Brenna had accomplished and discovered that she'd put plates around the table—that was all.

As she retrieved cutlery from the drawer, she didn't ask what her brothers were up to. While Maureen wouldn't hesitate to conscript her husband and sons if she needed their help, she generally considered the kitchen a woman's domain—not a woman's responsibility so much as her sanctuary.

When Fiona got back with the ice cream and Brenna managed to extricate herself from her phone, the

O'Reilly family gathered around the table. Conversation flowed freely and steadily as everyone piled their plates with the roast chicken, mashed potatoes and buttered corn, with topics ranging from ranch issues to town gossip.

Fallon hadn't been kidding when she told Jamie that attendance at Sunday night dinner was mandatory. Although the kids were adults now, they continued to live on the ranch. The girls still slept under their parents' roof, but the boys had converted an old barn into their own living quarters. Throughout the week, it was rare for all of them to be able to sit down at the same time, which was why Maureen and Paddy insisted on them all being together on Sunday.

After everyone had eaten their fill of dinner and dessert, Fiona went out to the barn with Paddy to check on her mare, who had stumbled while they were out riding earlier and had some minor swelling in her right foreleg. Keegan and Ronan headed to the barn, too, to complete the evening chores, and Brenna slipped away to visit her inconsolable friend. Which meant that the responsibility for clearing away the dishes and cleaning up the kitchen fell to Maureen and her youngest daughter.

Fallon didn't mind the chores or hanging out with her mother. Unlike some of her friends, she had a good relationship with both of her parents and she felt fortunate that there wasn't anything she couldn't talk to them about.

Unfortunately, it also meant that her parents didn't consider any topics off-limits. After she'd filled the sink with soapy water and started to wash the pots and pans, Maureen said, "I don't think you should continue to take care of the Stockton triplets."

"What?" Fallon picked up a towel and turned to look at her mother. "Why would you say something like that?"

"Because I'm worried about you," Maureen admitted.

"You don't need to worry," she told her. "I'm fine."

"You're exhausted."

"I'm a little tired," she acknowledged. Okay, she was a lot tired, but that wasn't the sole responsibility of Jamie or his babies. And while her days were busy, she would rather give up her job at Country Kids Day Care than give up a single minute of the time that she spent at The Short Hills Ranch. Especially if that brief, almost-kiss Jamie had given her was a prelude to better things.

"And when was the last time you were on a date?" Maureen asked.

Fallon frowned at the question. "What does that have to do with anything?"

"You don't even know, do you?" her mother challenged.

"It's been awhile," she admitted, because the truth was, she couldn't remember the last time she'd been out on a date. But not dating didn't mean she was missing out on anything, either, especially since the last few dates that she'd had were obviously not very memorable.

In fact, feeling the touch of Jamie's lips on her cheek had affected her more deeply than any other man's kiss had ever done. Or maybe it was the anticipation that had tied her insides up in knots. Because for a brief moment, she'd actually thought that he was really going to kiss her. The way his gaze had dropped to her mouth and lingered there, she'd been almost certain he intended to touch his lips to her own.

But, of course, he hadn't. Because Jamie didn't see her as a woman but as a friend.

"Because every free minute you have is spent taking care of Jamie Stockton's babies," her mother continued, oblivious to the direction of Fallon's wandering thoughts.

"I'm not the only one who helps out," she felt compelled to point out. "There are at least half a dozen people who are still part of the baby chain."

"I know," her mother acknowledged. "But you spend more hours over there than anyone else, except maybe Jamie's sister, who lives there."

"Because I have more time than anyone else. Cecelia Pritchett and Margot Crawford both have husbands waiting for them at home at the end of the day. Paige Dalton has a husband and a baby."

"Which is exactly my point," Maureen said gently. "The other women have husbands and/or children of their own. And soon Bella is going to be married, too. But as long as you make Jamie Stockton and his babies your priority, you're never going to find a man to marry and raise a family with."

"Considering that I'm only twenty-four, it might be a little premature to slap the 'old spinster' label on me," she said lightly.

"You were twenty-three when you started helping with the triplets," her mother noted. "And you'll be twenty-seven before they're ready for preschool. And maybe that is still young, but not as young as many of the women who have recently moved to Rust Creek Falls looking to marry handsome cowboys."

"I appreciate your concern, but there's no reason to

worry about me," she insisted. "Besides, Jamie's planning to start the babies in day care in the New Year."

"Well, I think that's a good idea," Maureen said. "For a lot of reasons."

Fallon nodded, because she knew her mother was right. But she also knew she was going to miss HJK—and their father—terribly when she wasn't seeing them four times a week.

"Speaking of good ideas, Presents for Patriots is coming up," her mother reminded her.

Fallon wasn't sure that was a natural segue, but she was happy enough about the shift in topic that she didn't question it. "I'll be there."

"Good. It's a popular community event."

"I'm aware of that," she acknowledged.

"And it might be a good opportunity for you to meet some single men," her mother pointed out.

"Really, Mom? You want me to hook up with some guy at a local gift-wrapping event?"

Maureen flushed guiltily. "I'm not suggesting a hookup."

"I didn't realize you were so eager to marry me off," Fallon said. She didn't dare tell her mother that she'd already invited Jamie to attend the event with her. She knew that he didn't like to go into town except if absolutely necessary, because he was weary of the pitying glances he always received. But she wanted to coax him out of his comfort zone, get him involved in something for the community.

"I'm not trying to marry you off," her mother denied. "I just want you to be happy. You're working at Country Kids because you love children—and I know that's one of the reasons you were so quick to sign up for the baby chain when Bella was looking for volunteers."

Fallon opened a cupboard to put away the pots and lids she'd finished drying.

"You're not asking me what I think the other reasons are," her mother noted.

"Jamie and Bella have been friends of mine since we were all kids."

"That's true," Maureen acknowledged. "It's also true that you've had a crush on Jamie for a lot of years."

She kept her face averted so her mother wouldn't see the color that flooded her cheeks. "That was a long time ago—before he went away to college."

"And you were devastated when you found out that he was marrying Paula," her mother said gently.

"And all this time, I thought I'd done a pretty good job hiding my true feelings."

"You did. From everyone else. But a mother knows when her child is hurting," Maureen said. "And it hurts a mother, too, when there's nothing she can do to help."

"Well, I got over it," Fallon told her.

"Did you?"

She sighed. "Okay—I'm trying to get over it."

"Do you really think that's going to happen when you see him three or four times a week?" Her mother pulled the plug in the sink to drain the water, then turned to face her daughter. "Or are you hoping that seeing *you* three or four times a week is going to somehow change Jamie's feelings for you?"

"Maybe I am," she finally acknowledged.

Maureen brushed a strand of hair away from her face, tucking it behind her ear as she'd done so many times over the years. "I'm not going to say it couldn't ever happen—because if the man had half a brain in his head, he'd be head over heels in love with you," she said. "Unfortunately, I think he's got so much going on in his life right now, he just can't see the beautiful, incredible woman who is in front of him, and I don't see his situation changing anytime soon."

Fallon nodded, accepting the truth of her mother's words.

"And I don't want you to miss out on falling in love with some other terrific guy who is capable of loving you the way you deserve to be loved because you're hung up on Jamie," Maureen continued.

She felt the sting of tears behind her eyes. She wished she could tell her mother to mind her own business, but she knew that her concern was sincere. And truthfully, Fallon wanted what her parents had—a loving, supportive relationship that had endured through five kids and thirty years of marriage.

Her mother was right—things were going to change in the New Year. Which meant that she had less than four weeks to get Jamie to see her as a woman instead of a friend. And if she had any hope of succeeding, drastic measures were required.

When Jamie made his way downstairs Monday morning, his gaze automatically went to the corner of the living room where the Christmas tree was standing. Though he wouldn't have thought it was possible, seeing it there did lift his mood a little. Or maybe seeing the tree made him think about cutting it down and decorating it with Fallon, and that was what lifted his mood.

He was still thinking about her as he rode the fenceline Monday afternoon, checking for any new problems, when he heard something unexpected. He strained to listen, but the sound—a whimper?—was too quiet and distant to ascertain the direction.

Or maybe it was just the wind that he'd heard.

But as he continued to ride, he heard it again. A low and plaintive sound.

Definitely not the wind.

"Do you hear that?" he asked his mount.

The mare tossed her head, as if in agreement.

"Should we check it out?"

He loosened the reins to let Willow take the lead, trusting that she would lead them in the right direction.

She turned toward the shelter he'd built for the expectant stray who had been hanging around the property.

That's where he found the puppies.

He scanned the horizon, looking for the mother, but she was nowhere to be found and the puppies sounded scared and hungry. Though they were huddled together for warmth, they weren't newborns. At least six weeks old, he guessed, which meant that if he scared them, they could—and likely would—scatter. And there was no way he could chase down six puppies.

His attention was snagged by a movement at the corner of the shelter.

Ah, hell—there were seven.

"Looks like you've got your hands full there," Brooks Smith said when he entered the exam room and saw the crate of puppies on the table.

"Not my hands," Jamie denied.

After he'd discovered them, he'd called his neighbor and asked if he could borrow a dog crate. While he didn't like to think that the mother had abandoned them, it was obvious the puppies were scared and alone and hungry, and there was no way he could leave them outside with the temperature steadily dropping. Dallas Traub had provided not just the crate but helped round up the animals so that Jamie could take them to the Buckskin Veterinary Clinic to be checked out.

He'd called ahead to let Brooks know that he was bringing in a whole litter of puppies, and the vet had apparently assumed they were his—an assumption he was eager to dispel. "I've seen a stray golden wandering around the north side of the property for the past several months—I'm guessing they belong to her. Or they did before she abandoned them."

"They weren't abandoned," Brooks told him.

"How do you know?"

"The mother was brought in yesterday afternoon by Gene Strickland. He and Melba were out for a drive yesterday and the dog darted out into the road in front of them. He slammed on his brakes but the vehicle didn't stop in time. Both Gene and Melba were devastated that the dog didn't make it. And though we could tell she was a nursing mother, we had no idea where to begin looking for her pups."

"So now they're orphans," Jamie realized.

Brooks nodded.

"How old?"

"Between six and seven weeks," the vet said, confirming Jamie's initial guess. "The mom was definitely a golden retriever but, looking at the puppies, I'd guess the dad was a shepherd."

"In other words—they're going to get a lot bigger than they are right now?"

"Probably between sixty to eighty pounds." Brooks made some notes in a file, then glanced up at Jamie again. "You thinking of keeping them?"

"No way," he said immediately. Firmly. "I can't. I've already got three babies." And the only way he was managing to take care of them was with a lot of help.

"I'll have Jazzy come in to take some pictures," he said. "We'll post an ad in the waiting room, another at Crawford's and maybe one at the community center."

Jamie nodded, because he agreed the vet's plan was the best idea.

But still he lingered, thinking that he'd always wanted a dog at the ranch. That a ranch needed a dog.

He looked down at the little bundle of fur that was attempting to climb up his leg, desperately trying to snag his attention. While its siblings were wrestling with one another, this one—the first one to tentatively come forward out of the makeshift shelter to sniff his boots—seemed eager for human contact.

Even though he knew he shouldn't, he reached down and scooped up the little guy, rubbing the soft fur beneath his chin with a knuckle. The puppy panted happily. "You're going to do just fine wherever you end up," he said.

"They'll find homes quickly," Brooks said. "Puppies always do."

Jamie nodded, but he made no move to put the little furball down.

"So if you're thinking that maybe you'd like to keep one, you'd better decide fast," his friend warned.

"I'd have to be crazy to take on the responsibility of a puppy," he said.

Brooks just grinned.

Jamie watched the other puppies playing together on the floor, attempting to climb over one another, chewing on ears and chasing tails. He knew it was ridiculous to hope that they would stay together. He couldn't imagine anyone wanting to take in seven puppies that would grow up to be seven fairly large dogs.

But maybe he could keep just one.

No. He immediately discarded the thought of tearing one of these adorable puppies away from its siblings. Maybe it wasn't a reasonable comparison, but he remembered how he'd felt when he'd been separated from his siblings after their parents had died. How lonely and alone he'd felt when they were gone. But at least he'd had Bella.

So how could he possibly keep one puppy and force it to say goodbye forever to its six siblings?

The answer was simple: he couldn't.

He also couldn't keep them all…but maybe he could find room for the little guy in his arms…and one more.

It was snowing again.

Fallon glanced at the clock and then out the window and tried not to worry too much about the fact that Jamie wasn't home. He'd sent her a quick text message more than an hour earlier, just saying that he'd needed to run an errand in town but shouldn't be long.

She didn't mind staying late, but the way the snow was blowing around outside, she was beginning to worry whether he would make it home at all. The eight to ten inches that had fallen last week had laid a pretty blanket of white on the ground, but the storm that was blowing through town now was hitting Rust Creek Falls with both fists and visibility was practically nonexistent.

Since he was going to be late, she'd fed the kids and put them in their play yard while she tidied the kitchen. A plate of leftover steak pie had been set in the oven to stay warm for Jamie when he got home. *If* he got home.

She glanced out the window again, exhaling a shaky sigh of relief when she saw, in the distance, a set of headlights turn into the drive. She checked on the babies again, then slid her hand into an oven mitt and removed Jamie's dinner from the oven.

She set the plate on the table, beside the bowl of salad, as she heard the creak of the back door opening. She heard him kicking the snow off his boots, then soft murmuring.

Puzzled by the quiet tone and words indecipherable over the howl of the wind, she glanced toward the door and saw him holding two tiny, furry bodies close to his chest.

Puppies.

The first one had butterscotch-colored fur with brown ears, white paws and a white tipped tail. The other had slightly darker fur, with a lighter patch around its muzzle and down its throat.

"Oh. My. God." The words were a whispered squeal of excitement. "They're beyond adorable."

He grinned. "They are, aren't they?"

She eagerly took the soft, wriggling bodies from his arms so that he could shed his coat and boots. The puppies, happy to make her acquaintance, tried to climb up her chest to swipe at her mouth with their tiny pink tongues. "You found them?" she guessed.

He nodded.

"And you're keeping them?"

"That's the plan," he admitted.

Fallon shook her head as she nuzzled the puppies. "You're crazy. You know that, don't you?"

"Quite possibly," he agreed.

"What do you think your sister's going to say when she comes home and finds you've added two puppies to your family?" Though the question was obviously intended as an admonishment, the effect was negated by her cuddling with and cooing over the puppies.

"She'll probably say that I'm certifiably insane," he guessed. "And then she'll take one look at them and fall head over heels in love—like you did."

Fallon didn't doubt it was true. Her friend had always loved playing with Duke when she hung out at the O'Reilly house, which she'd done as often as she could. Bella had confided in Fallon about her wish for a dog—although, in retrospect, Fallon suspected that what her friend had really wanted was the love and affection that a dog gave so readily and easily. Whatever her reasons, her wishes had been denied. Agnes and Matthew Baldwin had refused to allow any animals in their house.

"Yeah, she'll love the puppies," Fallon agreed. "But that doesn't preclude the possibility of her killing you."

"I can handle my sister," he assured her.

"I hope so."

The lights flickered as the windows rattled their protest against the howling wind.

"It sounds nasty out there," she noted.

He nodded. "That's another reason I'm so late—I could barely see two feet in front of the truck while I was driving home."

"Then I should head out before the storm gets worse."

"No," he said. "You should stay here tonight."

She'd been waiting a long time to hear those words, though whenever she'd imagined him saying them to her, it hadn't been because of unsafe road conditions.

But regardless of his reasons for issuing the invitation, there was only one answer she wanted to give. "Okay—I'll stay."

Chapter Seven

When Fallon called to let her parents know she would be staying at The Short Hills Ranch rather than drive home in the storm, she knew they would approve of her decision if not the situation. So she was relieved when Brenna answered the phone and told her that both Paddy and Maureen were out at the barn, alleviating any guilt about leaving the message with her.

She played with the puppies while Jamie spent some time with the triplets before he gave them their bath and got them ready for bed. Conscious of the fact that little puppies had little bladders, Fallon decided to take the pair of them outside. In the knee-deep drifts, she got no further than the corner of the porch, where she set the puppies down.

She was surprised—and grateful—that both puppies actually squatted and peed. When she scooped them up again, their little bodies were shivering, so she tucked them close to keep them warm.

She could smell the familiar comforting scent of wood-smoke when she stepped back inside the house and knew that Jamie had lit a fire in the hearth. The way the wind was howling, it wasn't just possible but likely that the house would lose power and though he had a generator—as most ranchers did—the fire would help keep the house warm so that he didn't have to use it for that purpose. He'd also set candles in holders around the room, although they remained unlit.

"Did you get in touch with your folks?" Jamie asked, when she set the puppies on the floor in the living room.

"I talked to my sister," she said.

"Good. I wouldn't want your family to think you were on your way home in this storm."

"What about Bella?" she asked. "Do you know where she is?"

He nodded. "Hudson took her to Maverick Manor for dinner, before the storm hit, so they've decided to spend the night there."

"Why do you sound so disapproving?"

"Because she's my little sister—and yes, I know that she and Hudson are engaged, but they're not married."

"And, of course, you never had sex with your fiancée before you were married?" she teased.

He winced. "Please. I do not want to even think that word in conjunction with my sister."

Fallon laughed. "Okay, big brother, I'll leave you with your delusions."

"Thank you," he said sincerely.

"I can't help but wonder, though…if you're this protective of your little sister, what are you going to be like when Katie is old enough to date?"

"I don't know," he admitted. "But at least I've got thirty years before I need to worry about that."

"Thirty years, huh?"

"At least," he confirmed.

"So maybe it's not unreasonable for my parents to worry about the fact that I'm spending the night here," she mused aloud.

"Why would they worry about you spending the night here?"

She felt her cheeks flush as she spelled it out for him. "Because you're a man…and I'm a woman."

"But they know me," he said. "And they know I would never take advantage of our friendship in that way."

"Thanks," she said dryly. "You sure do know how to boost a girl's ego."

"I didn't mean—" He scrubbed his hands over his face. "I'm going to go out and shovel off the porch and walkway, so that when Bella makes her way home in the morning, she'll hopefully be able to find her way to the door."

Fallon just nodded.

She knew that she had no right to be upset with him for saying aloud what she'd always suspected—that he didn't see her as a woman. But she was upset and frustrated, and now she was trapped under the same roof with him for the night.

After checking on the babies to make sure they were content and secure in their play yard, she headed upstairs to borrow a pair of pajamas from Bella's drawer. Poking through the cupboard of her friend's bathroom, she also found a new toothbrush that she appropriated for her own use. She hurriedly changed and cleaned her teeth, then headed back downstairs.

Since the power wasn't out yet, she decided to turn on the Christmas tree lights. And because she suspected that Jamie would want something to warm him up when he came inside—and because she couldn't seem to stop taking care of him even though she knew it was a habit she needed to break—she put on a pot of decaf coffee.

When Jamie returned, she was on the sofa with the babies beside her, reading a story to them. Though they rarely sat still for long, Fallon believed it was important to teach children an appreciation of books at an early age. Recently, she'd been reading them stories about Christmas—particularly books with pictures of Santa Claus so that he wouldn't seem like a complete stranger when they went to the mall in Kalispell to have their photo taken with him.

After a quick shower, Jamie came back downstairs wearing a pair of flannel lounge pants and a long-sleeve thermal tee that hugged his torso in a way that made her mouth go dry. Because no matter how many times she tried to tell herself that he was a friend, she couldn't stop seeing him as a man.

The only man she'd ever wanted.

Despite the storm still raging outside, it was undeniably cozy inside the house. Carrying a mug of the coffee that Fallon had brewed for him, Jamie paused in the arched entranceway of the living room, a fist squeezing his heart when his gaze settled on the Christmas card-worthy scene in front of him.

A brightly lit Christmas tree topped with a sparkling

star beside the stone fireplace with flames flickering in the hearth, a beautiful woman sitting cross-legged on the sofa with one baby in her lap and another on either side of her, reading aloud to them a story about Santa and a snowman. Looking at Fallon with Henry, Jared and Katie, he was overwhelmed by gratitude to her, for everything she'd done for his babies.

He felt a glimmer of something else, too—an awareness of Fallon as more than a childhood pal and favorite caregiver to his children, an appreciation of her as a beautiful and captivating woman. But he wasn't ready to acknowledge those feelings. He didn't want to see her as anything more than the steady and true friend she had always been.

Instead, he focused on the crucial role she'd played in the baby chain. He knew there was no way he would have made it through the past ten months without the community volunteers—and Fallon in particular. She'd gone above and beyond for him and his babies, taking care not just of their basic needs but lavishing them with attention and affection, loving them as easily and naturally as he would expect a mother to do. It didn't surprise him that Henry, Jared and Katie absolutely lit up whenever she was around, greeting her with big smiles and outstretched arms, vying for her attention. It did surprise him that her presence had the same effect on him, though he was careful not to show it.

Fallon finished the last page of the book and closed the cover.

"Now that's what I call a successful bedtime story," he told her.

She glanced at the babies cuddled against her and

discovered they were asleep. "One of these days, they'll stay awake until the end."

He set his coffee down on the table and picked up Jared and Henry, one in each arm. Fallon stood up with Katie in her arms and followed him up the stairs. Taking care of the babies was—if not easy, at least natural for her, and he knew that she would be a great mother someday. The kind of mother he'd always hoped his children would have.

When the babies were settled in their cribs, he stayed in their room for another minute, just watching them sleep. "I used to do this all the time when I first brought them home from the hospital," he confessed to Fallon. "Stand here watching them sleep and listening to them breathe, alternately thanking God for giving me three perfect babies and cursing Him for taking away their mother."

Fallon stood beside him, not saying anything, just listening to him talk.

"But it wasn't anyone's fault except Paula's," he admitted. "If she'd gone to her doctor's appointments, the preeclampsia would have been diagnosed, arrangements made for the safe delivery of the babies, and she would have lived." He shook his head. "I'll never understand why she skipped those appointments and jeopardized not just her life but our babies' lives, too."

"She didn't do it on purpose," Fallon said to him now. "Whatever her reasons for not having regular checkups, I don't think she truly understood the risk she was taking. If she had, if she'd even suspected how dangerous the consequences could be, she never would have done so."

"I wish I could believe that was true, but in those last few months, she was so angry with me."

"With you? Why?"

He only shook his head, because he couldn't repeat her words aloud. Not even to Fallon.

Thankfully, she didn't press him for a response. Instead, she laid her hand on top of his, curled over the side rail of Katie's crib, and squeezed it reassuringly. "Maybe you need to stop looking back and focus on the future and your babies."

"They're the reason I get up at way-too-early o'clock every morning," he admitted. "I need to make this ranch a success so I can provide for them. And yet, I spend so much time working, I feel as if I'm missing out on their childhood."

"You've mostly just missed out on a lot of dirty diapers," she teased.

He felt a smile tug at his lips, for just a moment. "I wouldn't have been able to keep them if I hadn't had the baby chain volunteers helping out every day." He lifted his eyes to hers. "I wouldn't have been able to do it without you."

"No one in this town would have let you lose your family."

Again, Jamie thought, but he didn't say the word aloud.

He didn't need to.

He sat up for a while with Fallon, talking about the upcoming holidays. She again hassled him about all the "great Christmas ideas" she'd enumerated on her list, such as visiting Santa, baking cookies, singing carols and taking part in the Candlelight Walk. Although he liked to tease her about her obsession with the holidays, he couldn't deny that she had a way of making everything fun. She found pleasure in the simplest things, and her pleasure was infectious. Over the past ten months, he hadn't found many reasons—aside from his babies—to smile. Being with Fallon made him smile.

When he finally headed upstairs to his bed, leaving her on the sofa with a pile of blankets, he found sleep elusive. Maybe it was because he'd been talking to Fallon about Paula earlier that thoughts of his ex-wife continued to linger in his mind. But Fallon was the only person he could talk to about so many things. As a result, she knew almost all of his secrets. She certainly knew more about the problems in his marriage than anyone else, but even she didn't know everything...

Moving to rural Montana had been a major adjustment for his Seattle-born wife, but during her first summer in Rust Creek Falls, she'd made an effort to meet people and fit into the community. During that time, he was working almost from sunup to sundown, trying to take care of the ranch without relying too much on outside help he couldn't really afford.

But after they'd been married almost a year, he'd broached the idea of starting a family. They hadn't talked about children before they were married, because he hadn't thought such a discussion was necessary. In his mind, a wedding was a natural prelude to a family.

But when he suggested that they could stop using birth control, Paula balked. As far as she was concerned, their life was perfect and adding a child to the mix could mess up everything. Besides, she wasn't really the maternal type, anyway.

Jamie had been stunned. How could she possibly

think that a baby would mess up anything? And why would she question her motherly instincts? Rather than actually answer any of his questions, Paula agreed to stop taking her birth control pills to "see what happens."

And Jamie, excited by the prospect of having a child with his wife, didn't push for answers because he believed that, when they finally had a baby together, she would see that all of her worries and concerns had been for naught.

Except that another six months went by and *nothing* happened. He'd always envisioned himself having a house full of children—like the loving home his parents had provided before their deaths—and he wasn't prepared to give up on that dream. Instead, he suggested that they make an appointment with a fertility specialist. Paula agreed, albeit with obvious reluctance.

By that time, he'd realized there was more going on than his wife was telling him, but he still believed they could work through whatever was bothering her. Until a few days before the wedding of Braden Traub and Jennifer MacCallum, when he was searching for a pair of tweezers to remove a splinter from his thumb and found a package of birth control pills hidden in a zippered compartment in his wife's makeup case.

"I shouldn't have lied to you," she admitted, swiping at her tears with the back of her hand. *"But I was afraid that, if I got pregnant and fat, you wouldn't want me anymore."*

He was sincerely baffled by her response. *"Why would you ever think any such thing?"*

"Because that's what happened in my parents' marriage, when my mom got pregnant with me."

"*Whatever problems your parents had, had nothing to do with you,*" *he assured her.*

But she shook her head. "*Everything was fine, until I came along. They were happy and in love, and then her body started to grow and change, and my dad lost interest. That's when he started looking at other women—and sleeping with other women. And I didn't want to risk the same thing happening to us.*"

Jamie's heart ached for her: the little girl who had felt responsible for the problems in her parents' marriage, and the woman who believed that he would ever be unfaithful to her. And though he felt he understood her better now, he wasn't sure he could forgive her actions. She'd lied to him—for more than a year, every time they'd made love, every time he'd asked about her cycle, she'd deliberately and continuously lied to him.

"*When I promised to love, honor and cherish you, I meant every word of it,*" *he said, then dropped the package of pills on the desk and turned away.*

She pushed away from the desk and rushed toward him. "*Please, Jamie. Give us another chance to be a family.*"

Of course, those words wrapped around his heart like a lasso over the head of an errant calf, and yanked him right back into line.

And then Paula took his hand and led him to the bathroom, where she dumped the pills into the toilet and flushed them all away.

Jamie knew that the issues between them couldn't be solved that easily, but he let himself believe that it was the first step toward getting their life back on track.

And when they attended Braden and Jennifer's wedding a few days later, he couldn't help but remember their wedding day, when they were head over heels in love and confident in their future together. Listening to the exchange of vows reminded him of the promises that he and Paula had made to one another, and he knew that he owed them a second chance.

When they went home after the wedding, they were both drunk on love and intoxicated by joy, and they made love all through the night. It wasn't until several weeks later that he heard about the spiked wedding punch and realized they might have been drunk on more than love. Regardless of the reasons, that night signaled a turning point in their relationship—the new start they both claimed to want.

Four weeks after the wedding, after Paula had been feeling dizzy and sick for about a week, Jamie encouraged her to take a pregnancy test.

The test was positive, and he was ecstatic. His wife was a little less so, but she seemed willing to believe his promises that they would have a wonderful life together with their baby. Then she found out that there wasn't just one baby—there were three.

And the bigger Paula's belly grew, the more miserable she became. She refused to let him accompany her to her monthly check-ups, insisting that he'd done enough. Maybe he should have insisted, but the truth was, by that time, he was weary of the arguing and bickering, so he relented and let her go to the doctor's appointments on her own. Because it never occurred to him that she wasn't going.

And she never missed out on an opportunity to remind him that having three babies was *his* choice not hers.

He'd wanted to believe that as soon as their babies

were born and she held them in her arms, she would love them as much as he did.

Unfortunately, she'd never had that chance.

Chapter Eight

Fallon hadn't slept very well. Despite the fact that it was late when Jamie said good-night and finally turned out the lights, she'd had trouble falling asleep. Because as soon as she closed her eyes, she pictured Jamie upstairs in his bedroom. Alone in his big bed. And though she would never dare tiptoe up the stairs and crawl beneath the covers with him, there was no denying that she wanted to. The tantalizing thought teased her mind and stirred her body, and when she finally did sleep, she dreamed of him.

And then she'd awakened twice in the night to howling winds that rattled the windows and urged her to add more wood to the fire. So far, the power had not been lost, but better safe than sorry. She'd awakened three more times to put the puppies outside.

Jamie had lined a laundry basket with a towel for

them to sleep in, and Fallon had set the basket close by so that they wouldn't feel abandoned and alone. As a result, she'd heard every soft cry and whimper and, worried that every little sound might be an indication of a full bladder, she'd scooped them up, shoved her feet into her boots, and taken them out onto the porch.

The last time she'd ventured out into the frigid air, the first light of dawn was just starting to shimmer on the horizon.

She'd obviously fallen into a deeper sleep after that, because she didn't hear anything else until a warm, masculine voice whispered close to her ear.

"Wake up, Sleeping Beauty."

And she did—jolting awake and abruptly upward, the top of her head smacking Jamie in the chin.

She winced, he swore.

"Ohmygod. I'm so sorry."

He dropped to his knees beside the sofa and rubbed his chin. "I don't think you broke anything, but damn, you have a hard head."

"And you have a hard jaw," she told him, rubbing the top of her head.

He carefully wiggled the disparaged part of his anatomy.

"Are you okay?" she asked.

"I'm not sure. I think you might need to kiss it better."

She blinked, certain that she hadn't heard him correctly. "What?"

"When Jared fell down and banged his knee yesterday, you kissed it better."

"Well, yes," she admitted. "Because he's a baby."

"I bet my jaw hurts more than his knee," he told her.

Fallon rolled her eyes but leaned closer to brush her lips gently to his jaw, telling herself that it would be just like kissing Jared's knee. Except it was nothing like kissing Jared's soft, chubby knee. Jamie's jaw was hard and strong and rough with stubble that made her lips tingle, and he smelled like fresh hay and clean soap with an underlying hint of something that she recognized as uniquely his scent. Apparently he'd been out to the barn already, as he was every morning before the kids were even awake.

"Better?"

She drew back, but he was still close. Close enough that his lips were mere inches from her own. His gaze dropped to her mouth, lingered. She held her breath, waited.

"I think so," he finally said, and wiggled his jaw again.

Then he lifted a hand to her head, his fingers gently sifting through her hair in search of a possible bump. "How's the noggin?"

"I don't think I'm concussed," she said, trying to make light of the situation when just his nearness was making her heart race and her knees weak. Or maybe those were effects from the knock on her head.

"You're a dangerous woman," he teased.

"That's what all the guys say," she quipped back.

Despite the casual tone of their banter, there was something else in the air, something exciting and new and—

"It's like a Winter Wonderland out there," Bella announced, striding into the room.

It was a testament to how mesmerized Fallon had been by Jamie's nearness that she didn't hear any of the telltale signs of her friend's arrival. Apparently he'd been equally oblivious, because he quickly dropped his hand away and rose to his feet.

"How was the driving?" he asked his sister.

"Good," she said. "The plows must have worked through the night, because the roads are all clear."

"Which is my cue to be heading out," Fallon decided.

"You might want to change out of my pajamas first," her friend teased.

"Oh. Right." As she headed upstairs to do that, she heard Bella say to her brother, "That better not be a puppy in that laundry basket."

"Well, actually," he began.

And that was all Fallon heard before she closed the bathroom door.

Fallon wasn't surprised to find her mother sitting at the kitchen table with a cup of coffee on the table in front of her and a worried expression on her face when she walked in the door.

"Good morning," she said, kissing Maureen's cheek and hoping that her greeting would make it so.

The furrow between her mother's brows warned her otherwise. "I don't approve of you spending the night at Jamie Stockton's house."

"Did you really want me to drive home in the storm after the sheriff had made a public announcement asking all residents to avoid unnecessary travel?"

"Of course not," Maureen admitted. "I just wish you'd been home before the storm hit."

"That wasn't an option, because Jamie wasn't home before the storm hit."

"You know there will be talk if anyone saw your vehicle parked in his driveway overnight."

"People who want to talk will always find a reason to do so."

"Well, I'd prefer that they not talk about *my* daughter."

"You don't need to worry," Fallon assured her. "No one could have seen my SUV in Jamie's driveway because it was buried in snow."

"You shouldn't be so flippant about your reputation."

She sighed. "You can't have it both ways, Mom. Either Jamie is oblivious to the fact that I'm a woman, which all outward signs confirm, in which case there's no reason for you to fret about the fact that I spent the night under his roof."

"I don't fret," Maureen said, sounding a little miffed by the label her daughter had put on her concern.

"Or he's secretly but wildly attracted to me," she continued to make her point, "in which case you should worry that we spent all last night tearing up the sheets. But then your concerns that I'm wasting my time with a man who will never notice me are unfounded."

"When you have children of your own, you'll understand," her mother said.

Fallon sighed. "I know you're only looking out for me, Mom, which is why I'm going to tell you that absolutely nothing inappropriate happened and I spent the night looking after the puppies."

"What puppies?"

Having anticipated the question, Fallon already had her cell phone in hand to pull up the pics she'd taken of the puppies.

"Oh, my goodness." Maureen's voice was a whisper now. "Aren't they just the cutest things?"

"And there are five others who are just as adorable." She told her mother the story about how they came to be found on Jamie's ranch.

"Puppies are a lot of work—the housebreaking and obedience training," Maureen said, her tone a little wistful.

"Well, Brooks and Jazzy are keeping the others at the clinic until they can find good homes for them."

"I don't imagine they'll have to wait long."

"So you'd better make up your mind quickly," Fallon teased, knowing exactly what her mother was thinking.

"I'll talk to your father about it," Maureen decided. "I think he's been a little bit lonely since old Duke died." She looked up at her daughter then, a glint in her eye. "But don't think that story managed to distract me from our previous topic of conversation."

"I didn't imagine it would," she said, because her mother was like a dog with a bone when she got her teeth into a subject.

"And while you're busy taking care of another man's babies, the marriageable men of Rust Creek Falls are going out with other girls your age, falling in love and planning to marry them."

"Then clearly none of them were ever meant to be my husband."

"How can you possibly know that when you haven't gone out with any of them?" her mother challenged.

"This has been a really fun conversation," Fallon noted sardonically. "And as much as I'd love to continue it, I really need to shower and get ready for work."

Maureen immediately pushed her chair back from

the table. "Do you want me to make you some breakfast?"

As she grabbed a mug from the cupboard and filled it with coffee from the carafe to take upstairs with her, Fallon was reminded once again why she couldn't stay mad at her mother. Because whatever Maureen said or did, it was always with the best interests of her children in mind.

"Thanks," she said. "But I'm okay."

"Will you be home for dinner tonight?"

"If I ever get out of here, I will be home for dinner," she promised, and kissed her mother's cheek as she moved past.

Jamie had anticipated his sister's reaction to the puppies. He knew she'd be furious—for about two minutes. She'd chastise him for taking on more responsibility than he could handle, then he'd tell her the story of how he found them, and she'd cautiously lift one of them from the basket and fall head over heels in love.

What he didn't anticipate, after she'd gotten over being mad and the babies were dressed and fed and she was sitting with both of the puppies in her lap, was her completely out-of-the-blue comment: "There seemed to be a little bit of tension between you and Fallon earlier."

"What do you mean?"

She rolled her eyes. "You aren't really that oblivious."

"Oblivious to what?"

"Whatever's going on between the two of you."

"There's nothing going on between us," he said, deliberately blocking the tantalizing memories of soft lips and lace-covered breasts from his mind. "I've known Fallon forever—we're friends."

"That doesn't mean you can't be more."

"Neither of us is looking for anything more," he told her.

"Are you sure about that?" Bella challenged.

"Of course, I am."

She shook her head. "Then you're completely oblivious."

"Oblivious to what?"

"The way she looks at you," she said.

"She looks at me like everyone else in this town looks at me—with sympathy and pity."

"If that's what you see, then you're not very observant," his sister remarked.

"I know that she loves Henry, Jared and Katie," he said. "And I'm more grateful than I could ever express for everything she's done for my babies."

"Is that really all you feel—gratitude?" she asked, sounding a little disappointed.

"Of course not," he denied. "Aside from you, she's my best friend."

"Have you ever considered that you might be something more?"

"No," he said, but his gaze slid away as the memory of a long-ago kiss teased the edges of his mind.

"Well, maybe you should," Bella told him.

"I have my hands full enough with Henry, Jared and Katie—and now two puppies," he acknowledged. "The last thing I need is a woman in the mix."

"The fact that your hands are full with the babies is exactly why you should think about finding them a mother."

He flinched as if she'd struck him.

She immediately put a hand on his arm. "I'm sorry, Jamie. I didn't mean to sound insensitive."

He shrugged.

"I know that losing Paula devastated you, but you can't mourn her forever."

"It hasn't even been a year," he pointed out to her.

"I know," she said again, more softly this time.

But she didn't know all of it.

For example, she didn't know about the conversation that had taken place in the exam room when Paula had her first ultrasound.

"Is there a history of multiple pregnancies in your family?" the doctor asked, as he moved the wand over the barely-there curve of Paula's belly.

"No," the mom-to-be responded immediately, vehemently.

The doctor glanced at Jamie. "Your family?"

He shook his head, his gaze fixed on the monitor where he could clearly see the outline of not just one—and not even two—but three separate blobs.

"There's only one, right?" Paula asked, staring at the screen. "Something's wrong with your machine thing and the picture's broken, right?"

The doctor shook his head. "The machine isn't broken," he assured both of them, his tone calm and soothing. "You're pregnant with triplets."

Paula opened her mouth as if to reply, but closed it again without saying a word. And when she looked at him, her eyes were filled with fear and anger and tears.

"I can't have three babies," she told him. "I wasn't even sure that I wanted to have one."

"Well, it's not as if we really have a choice," he pointed out, determined to remain reasonable and calm

despite the fact that he was feeling a little bit of panic over the thought of three babies, too. But in addition to the panic, there was joy. A lot of joy.

"We do have a choice," she insisted. "We can reduce the number."

He stared at her, not wanting to comprehend what she was saying.

When he didn't respond, she turned to the doctor. "Doctors do it all the time, don't they?" she said to him—pleaded with him.

"Not all the time," he replied cautiously. "And not without a valid medical reason."

"My body can't possibly support three babies," Paula insisted. "Isn't that a valid medical reason?"

"There is no evidence to suggest that's true," the doctor denied.

In the end, she'd been right, but only because she hadn't made any effort to help her body support their babies.

That was the part of the story that no one knew, and Jamie wanted to keep it that way.

Fallon changed her mind at least half a dozen times on the trip from Rust Creek Falls to Kalispell. While the whole makeover thing had worked pretty well for Cinderella, she was less optimistic about her own prospects.

Yes, desperate times called for desperate measures and all that—but she didn't want anyone to know she was desperate. On the other hand, the conversation with her mother had made her face some hard facts, and the reality was that she had a very small window of opportunity to catch Jamie's eye. Maybe she was already too late, but with her self-imposed New Year's Eve deadline in mind, she took a deep breath, walked up to the counter of the fancy salon and said, "I need a makeover."

The girl seated at the computer—whose name tag identified her as Leila—barely glanced up from her phone as she continued texting. "What were you thinking? Hair? Nails? Makeup?"

"All of the above."

Leila reluctantly set aside her phone and shifted her attention to the computer screen. "We're currently booking for the middle of January. Is there a particular—"

"The middle of January?" Fallon interjected, her hopes immediately deflating. "Don't you have anything available today?"

The receptionist finally lifted her gaze to give the obviously despondent customer her full attention. "Honey, we're one of the top-rated salons in Kalispell and it's barely two weeks before Christmas."

Fallon released a weary sigh. "I'm guessing that's a no."

But Leila held up a hand—a silent request for Fallon to wait a moment—as she scrolled through the schedule displayed on her computer screen.

If Fallon couldn't get an appointment today, she didn't want one. And the middle of January was way too late to fit in with her plans.

"I almost forgot that we had a cancellation," the receptionist told her. "One of our top clients who regularly books a full array of services was scheduled to come in at twelve-thirty today, but her husband surprised her with an impromptu pre-holiday Mediterranean cruise."

Fallon held her breath. "I can have her appointment?"

Leila scanned the computer screen again. "Twelve-thirty with Cindy for hair," she confirmed. "Then Gina's available to do a mani-pedi at two, and Tansley can do your makeup after that."

"That all sounds perfect." She didn't even ask what it would cost—because she didn't care. If changing her outward appearance succeeded in finally getting Jamie Stockton to look at her like a woman instead of a pal, every penny would be money well-spent.

Fallon usually had her hair done at Bee's Beauty Parlor in Rust Creek Falls, where she got a family discount if Brenna washed and cut her hair. At La Vie Salon, the stylists had assistants who escorted clients from the waiting area—where orchestral music played quietly in the background and cold and hot beverages were offered to those lounging in the butter-soft leather chairs—to the prep area. There Fallon was turned over to a designated shampoo girl, who didn't just wash her hair but gave her scalp such an incredible massage she didn't ever want it to end. But of course it did, and when her hair was rinsed and conditioned and rinsed again, the assistant returned to escort her from the prep area to Cindy's work station.

After a brief introduction and a few minutes of general conversation that immediately put Fallon at ease, Cindy surprised her by asking, "What's his name?"

"Who?"

"The man." The stylist gently combed out her wet hair. "Whenever a woman comes in here for a make-over, it's usually because of a man."

Fallon wished she could lie. She didn't want to be the cliché, but Cindy's question confirmed that she was. And since she would probably never see this woman again, she confided the truth. "He's a friend who refuses to see me as anything but a friend."

"And you think—if you look different—he'll finally see you," the hair stylist guessed.

"I'm hoping," she admitted.

Cindy continued to snip the ends of her hair. "Do you realize how beautiful you are?"

She managed a wry smile. "I've been called cute, and occasionally pretty, but never beautiful."

"You are," the stylist insisted. "You've got those gorgeous blue eyes, which will be framed nicely with the wispy bangs I'm going to give you, and gloriously thick auburn hair."

"It's red."

"It's more than red. There are so many shades of copper and gold, and the curls—"

"The curls have to go," Fallon interjected.

Cindy looked horrified by the thought. "I think that would be a mistake."

"I need to look different," she said again. "If I don't get rid of the curls, he'll just think that I got my hair cut—if he even notices that much."

"This guy must be pretty special," the stylist said.

"He is."

"Then I'm going to do everything I can to help you knock his socks off," Cindy promised.

By the time Fallon walked out of the salon, she felt like a different woman—if not a less nervous one. When she stopped at the makeup counter to pick up some of the mascara and lip gloss Tansley had recommended, she did a double take when she saw her reflection in the mirror.

Although she'd given Cindy specific instructions on what she wanted—"to look different"—it still gave her a jolt to see how well the stylist had done her job. Yes, she'd had her eyebrows tweezed and her makeup done, but the biggest and most significant change was her hair. Without the mass of curls around her face, she almost looked like a completely different person.

And yes, that had been her purpose in requesting the makeover, but she found that she was nearly as apprehensive as she was excited about the changes. On the other hand, once she looked past the sleek curtain of hair and perfectly made-up face, she was still the same old Fallon in the same old plaid flannel shirt tucked into well-worn jeans with her favorite cowboy boots on her feet. If she wanted Jamie to see her as an attractive woman, she was going to have to overhaul her wardrobe, too.

Chapter Nine

He never should have agreed to this.

When Fallon had asked him to attend Presents for Patriots with her, Jamie should have declined the invitation. Instead, he'd said yes, partly because he'd long been a supporter of the event and partly because he had a hard time saying no to Fallon.

The original plan had been for him to pick her up so they could drive over together, but as he'd been getting ready to leave the house, Fallon had sent him a text message suggesting they meet at the community center because she was already out running errands.

Now he was here, but he didn't see her anywhere. He felt obviously and awkwardly alone and uncomfortable. Since the birth of the triplets and the death of his wife, he'd avoided trips into town as much as possible. Bella accused him of being an antisocial recluse, but he didn't agree with that assessment. If he chose to stay close to home, it was because of the responsibilities that he had there. It was also a convenient excuse to avoid the hushed whispers and pitying glances that seemed to follow his every step whenever he walked down Main Street.

Bella had been pleased when he'd told her that he would be attending the gift-wrapping event, and she'd immediately offered to stay home with HJK. While he appreciated her willingness to babysit and knew that his children adored Auntie Bella, he couldn't help thinking that he should be at home with them. Of necessity, much of his day was spent away from his kids so that he looked forward to spending any free time he had with them. And considering that the community center was rapidly filling up with volunteers, he didn't think he'd be missed if he decided to slip out the door.

Except that he'd promised Fallon he'd be here. And he was—but where was she?

He looked around again, but he still didn't see her. Of course, there was already quite a crowd gathered. It seemed that every year, there were more and more people who came out in support of the event. He recognized Tessa Strickland, looking pretty and pregnant, with her fiancé Carson Drake, and Dr. Jon Clifton with Dawn Laramie, obviously and happily in love.

Then a glimpse of copper hair snagged his attention, and he automatically turned. The color was exactly the same as Fallon's, and he'd never known anyone else whose hair was as pretty and shiny as a new penny. The woman was about the same height as Fallon, too, with the same slender build, but the similarities ended there. Instead of Fallon's tumble of curls, this woman's

hair was straight and sleek; instead of Fallon's custom-
ary—and eminently practical—jeans and flannel shirts,
this woman was wearing a short denim skirt with high-
heeled boots and a soft green sweater that molded to
her distinctly feminine curves.

Definitely an out-of-towner, he decided. Because no
Montana native would venture out on a frigid December night without long underwear. But even while he
shook his head at the woman's complete lack of common sense, he couldn't deny that her long, shapely legs
sure were a pleasure to look at.

As if sensing his perusal, the woman slowly turned
around. And Jamie's jaw nearly hit the floor when he
realized the woman he'd been ogling *was* Fallon.

But he'd never seen Fallon looking like *this* before.
She was hot enough to melt the snow on top of Falls
Mountain, and he could tell by the way several other
men in attendance were checking her out that he wasn't
the only one who thought so.

Justin Crawford whistled under his breath. "Is that
Fallon O'Reilly?"

"Yeah," Jamie reluctantly confirmed.

"She looks…different." The cowboy continued to
stare at her. "Hot."

"Yeah," he said again, not at all happy to realize it
was true. She was his friend—he didn't like the idea
of other guys ogling her. And he especially didn't like
to admit that *he'd* been ogling her, too.

He crossed the room to where she was chatting with
Nina Traub. She glanced over as he approached, her lips
curving in a familiar and welcoming smile.

Except that even her mouth looked different today—
slicked with something peach-colored and shiny. Some-

thing that tempted him to want to taste her lips. The hint of a distant memory teased the back of his mind. Of a sweet and innocent kiss that had stirred some not-so-sweet-and-innocent yearnings. Yearnings he'd ignored then and needed to again now.

With a brief wave of acknowledgment in his direction, Nina headed the opposite way.

His dark mood must have been reflected in his expression, because Fallon's smile slipped as he drew closer. "Is everything okay?" she asked.

"Everything's just—" his gaze dropped to her mouth again "—peachy."

"Then why are you scowling?"

His only response was to shrug out of his jacket and drape it over her shoulders.

His action made her scowl, too. "What are you doing?"

"It's cold in here," he told her, inwardly cursing the fact that his jacket barely covered the curve of her butt. It certainly didn't come close to the hem of her short skirt—or the mile of shapely leg on display beneath that hem.

"I'm not cold," she said, pulling his jacket off her shoulders and holding it out to him.

He took her arm instead of the jacket.

"Come on," he said, and guided her over to a vacant table. He held out a chair for her to sit down, so that her legs would be hidden from view beneath the table.

"What's going on with you?" she asked him.

"I've been waiting half an hour for you to show up," he said, which was a slight exaggeration and not even close to being the reason for his irritation.

"Sorry," she said. "I was in Kalispell today and ran into some traffic getting back."

"What were you doing in Kalispell?"

Fallon looked at him for a long minute, then shook her head. "Apparently I wasted a lot of time and money."

"Shopping?" he guessed.

"That, too," she agreed, managing to keep her tone light despite the fact that his obliviousness had caused her ever-hopeful and pathetic heart to sink into the pit of her stomach.

"For Christmas?" he guessed, because apparently this inane conversation wasn't yet close to being done.

"Actually, most of my Christmas shopping is done and my gifts wrapped," she told him. "I was looking for an anniversary present for my parents. They're celebrating thirty years of marriage on Christmas Eve."

"That's impressive," he said.

She nodded. And proof that her mother was obviously a lot more knowledgeable than Fallon when it came to matters of the heart. *If the man had half a brain in his head, he'd be head over heels in love with you. Unfortunately, I think he's got so much going on in his life right now, he just can't see the beautiful, incredible woman who is in front of him, and I don't see his situation changing anytime soon.*

Fallon had thought—hoped—she could change it. She'd honestly believed that changing her hairstyle, putting on some makeup and buying new clothes would make him look at her differently. A five-minute conversation had disabused her of that notion.

They worked together wrapping the gifts that were piled beside their table. Jamie didn't say much as they worked. Fallon found herself humming along to the

Christmas music that played softly in the background. There were a lot of people in attendance to help out with the event and much happy chatter as people talked with their friends and neighbors while they worked.

Jamie hardly said a word, and when he did speak, it was only to ask her to pass the scissors or tape.

"How were the kids today?" she asked, attempting to break the unexpectedly awkward silence.

"Good." He folded the corner of the paper, secured it with a piece of tape, and didn't look up at her.

"How is Jared doing with his new teeth?" she asked, having noticed that the little guy's first two teeth had finally broken through his bottom gums a few days earlier.

"Fine." Fold. Tape. Repeat.

"Are the puppies still sleeping in the laundry basket?"

"Fine," he said again.

She affixed a bow to the present she'd finished and set it aside. "You're not listening to anything I'm saying, are you?"

Now, finally, he glanced up. "What?"

She huffed out a breath. "If you don't want to be here, why did you agree to come?"

"I do want to be here," he said.

"Well, you're not acting like it," she told him.

"I'm just…thirsty."

She blinked. "You're thirsty?"

He nodded. "I'm going to grab a cup of hot apple cider. Do you want one?"

Though she was as baffled by his sudden interest in a beverage as she was by his lack of communication, she decided that cider would be good. "Sure," she agreed.

Jamie pushed his chair back and stood up to head toward the refreshment table.

Shaking her head at his inexplicable mood, she returned her attention to her task. Or pretended to, while she surreptitiously watched Jamie move across the room. There was just something about the way the man filled out a pair of jeans that made her blood hum in her veins. But she was tired of being a solo act. She wanted to be with a man who wanted to be with her, and since that obviously wasn't Jamie Stockton, she should follow her mother's advice and start looking in another direction.

Jamie hadn't quite reached the refreshment table when Bobby Ray Ellis slid into the chair he'd recently vacated.

She'd gone to high school with Bobby Ray and they'd occasionally hung out together in a group of friends, but they'd never dated. Probably because, like most of the other guys in Rust Creek Falls, he'd seen her as a good pal rather than a potential mate. And that had never bothered her before, because she'd been too infatuated with Jamie to want to go out with anyone else.

But now she was starting to accept that her mother was probably right. That it was time to give up hoping that Jamie would ever see her as anything more than a friend for himself and a babysitter for his children.

"You look awfully pretty tonight, Fallon," Bobby Ray said, drawing her attention back to the table.

She smiled, grateful that *someone* had noticed the effort she'd gone to with her appearance. "Thank you, Bobby Ray."

"And I was wonderin'," he continued, "if you've been dating anyone recently. Exclusively, I mean."

She shook her head as she cut a piece of paper from the roll. "No," she said, not wanting to admit that she hadn't been dating at all—exclusively or not.

"Because I wouldn't ever want to encroach on someone else's territory," he assured her, "but I sure would like to take you out sometime, if you were interested in goin' out with me."

And while a part of her bristled at the idea of being considered any man's "territory," she knew Bobby Ray too well to be offended by his choice of words. "Are you asking me out on a date, Bobby Ray?"

"Yes, ma'am, I am. Or at least, I'm tryin' to."

"I don't know what to say," she admitted.

"I can help you with that," he said. "Say yes."

She smiled at his polite earnestness. He really was a good guy and more than pleasant to look at. Maybe he didn't make her heart feel all fluttery inside, but since no one other than Jamie had ever had that effect on her—and since Jamie had shown less than zero interest in asking her out—she decided to follow her mother's advice and go out with other people. "Okay, yes," she finally agreed.

Bobby Ray's smile stretched across his face. "How about tomorrow night? They're showin' *National Lampoon's Christmas Vacation* at the high school."

Despite the impressive growth of the town in recent years, Rust Creek Falls still didn't have an actual movie theater. Instead, movies were shown on Friday and Saturday nights at the local high school. "That sounds like fun," she decided.

"Great. Give me your number and I'll get in touch with you in the mornin' to firm up plans," he said.

So she added her number to the contacts list in his phone as he did the same to hers.

Her former classmate had just slipped away when Jamie came back carrying two paper cups of hot apple cider. "What did Bobby Ray want?"

She accepted the cup Jamie offered and wrapped her hands around it, because maybe it was a little chilly in the room and tights weren't nearly as warm as long johns. "He asked me to go out with him."

Jamie scowled. "Like on a date?"

"You don't have to sound so surprised," she told him. "I do occasionally go out." Which okay, was a bit of a stretch considering that she hadn't had a date in more than a year. Still, his question and tone were both a little insulting.

"But... Bobby Ray?" he said skeptically.

"Why shouldn't I go out with Bobby Ray?" she challenged.

"He just doesn't seem like your type."

"Really? Then who do you think *is* my type?"

She held her breath, waiting for his response. Waiting for some hint that he'd finally recognized that they should be together.

But he only lifted a shoulder, a casual gesture of indifference. "I don't know."

She was oh-so-tempted to pick up the roll of wrapping paper from the table and whack him upside the head. Was he being deliberately obtuse? Or was he trying to let her down easy? Well, to hell with that.

"Just because you don't find me attractive doesn't mean that other men don't," she told him.

His scowl deepened. "What are you talking about?"

She shook her head. "Nothing. Forget it." She fought

against the tears that burned the backs of her eyes. "I think I'm going to go home now."

"What?" He seemed genuinely startled by her sudden announcement. "Why?"

"Because it's been a long day and I'm tired." And she knew that if she didn't make her escape quickly, she would likely do something she would regret—though it was a toss-up as to whether that "something" might be hitting him with the wrapping paper roll or kissing him senseless.

"But… I thought we were going to wrap presents together."

She pushed her chair away from the table. "There are enough other people here that I won't be missed."

Jamie watched her pull on her coat—a heavy, full-length garment that covered from her chin to the top of her boots—and wondered why he felt as if she'd directed that last comment at him. As he watched her go, he couldn't shake the feeling that he'd done something wrong, even if he had no idea what that something might be.

And though he'd only been fifteen years old when he lost his parents, they'd made a point of teaching him manners and responsibility, and it was all too easy to imagine what they'd say about him allowing Fallon to walk out into the darkness of the night alone.

He pushed his chair back and hurried after her.

The night was cold—the type of cold that seared the lungs and crunched beneath the feet. It did both as he jogged across the parking lot in an effort to catch up with her hurried stride.

"Fallon, wait."

"It's too cold to stand around outside," she told him, not even adjusting her pace.

"Let me apologize."

She paused beside her SUV and stuffed her hands into the pockets of her long coat. "Why do you think you need to apologize?"

"I don't know," he admitted. "But obviously I said or did something to upset you, and I'm sorry."

She shook her head. "No," she said, maybe a little sadly. "You didn't do anything."

"Fallon," he tried again.

She waited, expectantly, but he didn't know what else to say.

After a moment, she opened the door of her vehicle and stepped up onto the running board. "Good night, Jamie."

He moved closer and caught the top of the door before she could close it. "Bobby Ray's a good guy," he finally said.

She nodded. "I know."

"And if you really want to go out with him…well, I hope you have a good time."

She responded by shoving her key in the ignition and starting the engine—a clear indication that their conversation was over.

Have a good time.

Fallon drove home with Jamie's parting words echoing in her head and tears stinging her eyes. But she refused to let them fall. She refused to let herself cry any more tears over a man who was too blinded by his responsibilities and grief and guilt to see that she was in love with him.

There had been moments over the past couple of weeks—when he'd held her steady as she tried to loop the lights around the Christmas tree and when she'd kissed his chin after bashing it with her head—that she'd been certain he felt *something*. If not desire at least awareness. But apparently she'd been wrong about that, too.

And maybe she should be grateful that he'd never figured out the true depth of her feelings. Because as much as it hurt to acknowledge his disinterest, she knew it would be infinitely more painful to accept his pity.

She was almost home before she remembered that Bella had asked her to keep an eye open at the community center for any single women who might be interested in marrying Jamie and becoming an instant mother to his three babies. It wouldn't be too difficult to come up with a list of names for her friend. There were a lot of suitable candidates and many of them had been at Presents for Patriots tonight to check out the unmarried men in attendance—including Jamie Stockton.

Hadley Strickland was the first name that came to mind. Hadley was a beautiful young veterinarian from Bozeman who was visiting with her grandparents—Melba and Old Gene—over the holidays. She'd also spotted a couple of women she didn't know by name but who she guessed were cousins of the Daltons and definitely pretty enough to snag any man's attention. It certainly wouldn't take much effort for her to generate a list for Bella, but that didn't mean she was going to do it. She'd stood back and felt her heart shatter as Jamie married another woman once already. She wasn't masochistic enough to want to experience the same thing again.

* * *

"You weren't gone very long," Bella said, when Jamie walked into the house before nine o'clock. She was sitting on the sofa with Jared in her arms; both Henry and Katie were on a blanket spread out on the rug, sleeping. The puppies, confined to the play yard, immediately started jumping up at the walls of the enclosure, yipping for attention when he entered the room.

"There were a lot of people there. They didn't need me," he told her, scooping up the puppies before they woke the sleeping babies.

"But I thought you were meeting Fallon there."

"I was. I did."

"So where is she?" Bella asked.

"She went home."

His sister continued to rub circles on Jared's back. "Did something happen between the two of you?"

"Nope." He lowered himself into an armchair and lifted his feet onto the coffee table.

Bella narrowed her eyes. "What aren't you telling me?"

"Nothing."

She waited.

"I can't figure her out," he admitted. "She shows up looking like a completely different person, and half the guys there are drooling over her as if they'd never seen her before. And she's smiling at them and flirting with them. Bobby Ray even asked her out on a date—and she said yes."

"Does that bother you?"

"No," he lied. "Why would it bother me? She can date whoever she wants."

"Then why are you yelling at me?"

"I'm not yelling," he denied.

But when Katie lifted her head, he knew that his annoyance had been reflected in his volume.

"And what do you mean—she looked like a different person?" his sister pressed.

He set the puppies down again and picked up his daughter, rubbing her back until her eyes drifted shut again.

"Her hair," he finally responded to Bella's question in a quieter tone. "And her face. And her clothes."

"Could you be a little more specific?" she suggested, not even attempting to hide her amusement.

"She was wearing a skirt," he muttered, unable to banish the image of those endlessly long, shapely legs from his mind.

"A skirt?" Bella feigned shock. "I didn't know those were legal in Montana."

"A short skirt," he clarified.

She gasped. "Maybe we should call the sheriff."

"I'm glad you think this is funny," he said, though he wasn't glad at all.

"I don't think the situation is funny. I think your extreme response to the situation is funny."

He scowled at that.

"Fallon's decision to alter her appearance a little isn't cause for concern," she said gently. "And you need to realize that not all change is bad."

"She's going out with Bobby Ray," he said again, for some reason unable to get past that fact. "They've been friends since high school, and suddenly she's going on a date with him tomorrow night."

"No relationship is stagnant," Bella pointed out to him.

"But dating a friend—" He shook his head. "It seems to me an easy way to ruin a friendship."

"I guess that's why Fallon's going out with Bobby Ray and not with you," she said, pinning him with a look. "Because you wouldn't ever cross that line, would you?"

Chapter Ten

"I thought he was exaggerating," Bella said, her gaze skimming over her friend, from the top of her head to her toes and back again. "When Jamie came home last night, babbling about your hair and face and clothes, I actually thought he was making a big deal out of nothing."

"And now?" Fallon asked, wanting her friend's honest opinion of her makeover.

"Now I think I owe him an apology," Bella said.

"But what do you think of my new look?" she prompted.

"I think you look fabulous. Not that you don't usually look fabulous—because you do," her friend hastened to clarify. "But this is a very different look."

"Good. I wanted something different."

"But...why?" Bella asked.

"Because I'm tired of looking the same—and of everyone else looking at me the same way."

"*Everyone* else?" her friend queried. "Or *someone* in particular?"

Fallon had always wondered if her friend suspected that she had deeper feelings for Jamie than friendship, but if she did, she'd never voiced those suspicions aloud. So maybe this was a hint to Fallon that she could finally confide the truth to her friend. But before she could figure out how to say the words, Bella spoke again.

"Because I heard that Bobby Ray Ellis asked you out on a date."

She was surprised by her friend's remark. Not just the fact that Bella was somehow aware of her plans but the obvious enthusiasm in her tone. Almost as if she was steering Fallon toward Bobby Ray—and away from Jamie.

Was her friend trying to subtly warn her that the single dad was a bad bet? Or was Fallon reading too much into a simple comment?

"So…is it true?" Bella asked.

"It's true," Fallon confirmed. "We're going to see *National Lampoon's Christmas Vacation* tonight."

Her friend made a face. "At the high school?"

She nodded.

"That's not a real date," Bella lamented. "He could at least take you to an actual movie theater in Kalispell for a current feature."

"I like the *Vacation* movies," Fallon told her. "Besides, it's a long drive back from Kalispell if the date turns out to be a dud."

Her friend frowned. "But you don't think it will be a dud, do you? I mean, you do like Bobby Ray, right?"

"Sure," she agreed. "I mean, I've always liked Bobby Ray, even if I've never *liked* Bobby Ray."

"I'm confused," Bella said. "If you don't *like* him, why did you agree to go out with him?"

"Because he asked and I'm tired of sitting at home every night," she admitted.

"Then this whole makeover thing wasn't part of a plan to attract his attention?"

"No," Fallon said.

"But it was part of a plan to attract someone's attention," her friend guessed. "So whose?"

She shook her head. "It doesn't matter."

"Some guys are too blind to see what's right in front of their eyes," Bella said sympathetically. "And if your mystery man doesn't know how lucky he would be to have you, then it's his loss."

Fallon took her time getting ready for her date with Bobby Ray. Though he wasn't the man she wanted to be going out with, his apparent interest was a balm to her wounded ego and she wanted to repay him by showing that he was worth the effort to look nice.

She wore a knitted sweater with a low V-neck over a lacy camisole and another skirt, but this one was much longer, falling to mid-calf. Bobby Ray wasn't quite as tall as Jamie, but he was still several inches taller than her so she didn't worry about her cowboy boots adding an inch to her five-foot-eight-inch height.

She straightened her hair with the iron she'd bought for that purpose and carefully applied her makeup. A light dusting of powder to even out her complexion and mute the sprinkling of freckles across the bridge of her nose, some mascara to lengthen and darken her lashes and peach gloss to highlight her lips. After only a brief moment's hesitation, she spritzed on some of her favorite perfume.

The way that Bobby Ray's eyes lit up when she descended the stairs told her that he appreciated the effort. Her mother, too, smiled her seal of approval. In fact, she'd been overjoyed ever since Fallon had told her of the upcoming date. "I knew you'd meet someone if you made an effort to put yourself out there. And Bobby Ray is such a nice boy," she'd said.

She ushered them out now and waved goodbye to them from the door.

"Sorry about my mom," Fallon apologized as Bobby Ray pulled out of the driveway. "I haven't dated much in the past year and tonight has given her renewed hope that I won't die a spinster."

Bobby Ray chuckled. "I think you've got a few years before you need to worry about becomin' a spinster."

"She worries anyway—for some reason, more about me than my sisters, who are both older," she admitted.

"Well, I'm really glad you agreed to go out with me tonight," Bobby Ray said. "Even if it was only to appease your mother."

"It wasn't to appease my mother at all," she denied. "I was happy to accept your invitation."

"When I saw you at Presents for Patriots, I wasn't sure if I'd be steppin' on any toes by askin' you out."

She shook her head. "You definitely didn't step on any toes."

"Well, you were there with Jamie Stockton," he noted. "And I know you spend a lot of time helpin' out with his kids, so I thought maybe you and he were like…a couple."

"No." She shook her head. "We're just friends."

"That's good," he said. "Because he's a good guy, and I know he's had some hard knocks, so I didn't want to poach but I really wanted to ask you out."

He was right. Jamie was a good guy, and he had been dealt some hard knocks—and she was tempted to deal him another one to his thick skull, but she'd accepted that she couldn't make him acknowledge feelings that didn't exist.

"Now, I have a question I want to ask you," she said to Bobby Ray.

"Shoot."

"Was it the new hairstyle or the skirt that made you ask me out?"

"That's a pretty direct question," he said, the tips of his ears turning red. "Probably both. I mean—I always thought you were pretty, but we've known each other for so long, I didn't ever see you like a girl I'd want to go out with, until you looked different. If that makes any sense."

"It does," she agreed. And it was, after all, the reason she'd decided to change her appearance. Unfortunately, the man she'd hoped would look at her differently still didn't seem to see her at all.

Bobby Ray parked his truck outside the high school and immediately came around to open her door for her. She was touched by the gesture, pleased to be treated like a lady.

He paid their admission at the table set up in the foyer, then they took their tickets and walked down the hall toward the gymnasium.

"Do you want popcorn?" he asked.

"I can't imagine watching a movie without it," she told him.

He grinned at that. "Me, neither."

They lined up at the concession table, then carried their snacks and drinks into the makeshift theater.

She took off her coat and hung it over the back of her chair. "I'm just going to slip out to the ladies' room before the movie starts."

"I'll be right here," Bobby Ray promised.

She used the facilities, then washed her hands, exchanging pleasantries with a few other people she knew who came in while she was there—including Margot Crawford, Vanessa Dalton and Jordyn Clifton. On her way back to the gymnasium, she nearly bumped into the absolute last person she expected—or wanted—to see tonight: Jamie Stockton.

"What are you doing here?" she asked him.

He lifted one shoulder in a gesture of bafflement that matched the expression on his face. "Bella kicked me out."

Fallon frowned at that. "Your sister kicked you out of your own home?"

He nodded. "She said I needed to do something besides ranch chores and diaper changes, and since she knows that this is one of my favorite Christmas movies, she firmly nudged me in this direction."

"Are you here with anyone?" she asked, then held her breath while she waited for his answer.

He shook his head. "No. Just me."

Deeply ingrained manners warred with the instinct for self-preservation. On the one hand, she felt bad that he was alone. On the other, she was on a date. If she'd been with friends, inviting him to join them would be the polite thing to do. To invite him to sit with her and Bobby Ray would just be a whole lot of awkward—especially when Bobby Ray had already asked about her relationship with Jamie.

"Are you here with someone?" he asked.

She nodded. "Bobby Ray."

"Oh. This is your…uh…date?"

"Yes, Jamie. As inconceivable as it may seem to you, I am on a date."

He frowned. "I don't think it's inconceivable. I'm just… It doesn't matter," he decided. "And I should let you get back to your date. The movie's going to be starting soon."

She nodded. "And you need to find a seat. This movie seems to be a popular one."

Jamie smiled at that, and she inwardly cursed the skip of her pulse. Bobby Ray had a nice smile, too, and he was every bit as handsome as Jamie, but his smiles didn't affect her the same way. His nearness didn't make her feel hot, and his touch didn't make her skin tingle. On the plus side, he'd never broken her heart, either.

"It's a Saturday night and the only movie in town," Jamie pointed out.

"True enough," she agreed. "Well…enjoy."

"You, too," he said.

As she made her way back to her seat, Fallon promised herself that she would enjoy the movie and Bobby Ray's company. And she hoped Jamie would find a seat far away on the other side of the gymnasium so she could forget he was even there.

But because he was only looking for one empty chair, he managed to snag a spot only a few rows back from where she and Bobby Ray were sitting. And she was aware of him, of his eyes on her, throughout the whole movie.

Of course, she was probably only imagining his scrutiny. After all, he'd made it clear that he had no interest in anything more than a platonic relationship with her.

When the movie finished, Fallon and Bobby Ray decided to go to Daisy's Donuts for a hot beverage. The café was a popular destination for the post–movie night crowd, and there were already several other people ahead of them in line when they got there. Fallon was relieved that Jamie wasn't one of them. She was also pleased to see Tessa Strickland, hand-in-hand with her fiancé, Carson Drake. The sheriff, Gage Christensen, and his wife, Lissa, as well as Jordyn and Will Clifton were also there, confirming her mother's claim that everyone in town was pairing up, falling in love and making plans for their futures.

And while she liked Bobby Ray well enough, Fallon couldn't imagine falling in love with him and marrying him. Or maybe she wasn't being fair. Maybe she couldn't see him as her future husband because she'd never let herself imagine anyone but Jamie Stockton in that role. And since Jamie had made it clear that he wasn't ever going to see her as a potential wife, she needed to erase that image from her mind and open herself up to other possibilities.

"Do you know what you want?" Bobby Ray asked, as they stepped up to the counter.

I want the man I love to love me back.

But of course the girl behind the counter couldn't serve that to her in a tall mug, so she ordered a café mocha instead. Bobby Ray ordered a regular coffee, and they carried their drinks to a narrow booth. While they sipped their hot beverages, they chatted casually about his ranch, her job at the day care, the movie they'd just seen and upcoming holiday plans.

"You seem preoccupied," Bobby Ray said to her, when she lifted her empty cup to her lips.

"I'm sorry," she said. "It's been a long week and I think I'm more tired than I realized."

"As long as it's not the company that's puttin' you to sleep."

"It's not the company at all," she promised.

"Then let's get you home," he suggested.

He was being so attentive and sweet and she really wanted to *like* him, but if tonight had served no other purpose, it had confirmed that her thoughts—and her heart—were elsewhere.

She looked over at him in the dim light of the truck. He really was a handsome guy. Tall, dark blond, deep green eyes and the broad shoulders that came from honest physical labor. He'd been popular in high school and had dated a lot of girls before he hooked up with Jillian Landers at the beginning of their junior year.

For the last two years of high school, they'd been pretty much inseparable and everyone expected an engagement announcement would follow soon after their graduation. Instead, Jillian had run off to Billings with someone else.

Curious, and a little bit wary of picking at a scab over old wounds, she asked, "Do you ever hear from Jillian Landers?"

Bobby Ray seemed surprised by the question, but after only a brief hesitation, he said, "We keep in touch on Facebook."

"Is she still in Billings?"

He nodded. "Married with three kids already and a fourth on the way."

"Why aren't you married, Bobby Ray?"

"Is that a hypothetical question or a proposal?" he teased, not taking his eyes off the road in front of him.

"A purely hypothetical question," she assured him.

He shrugged. "I guess I never met anyone else who made me want to take that next step."

She nodded her understanding.

"Now it's your turn," he said. "Why aren't you married?"

"Probably the same reason," she said. Then she surprised herself as much as him by confiding, "Or maybe because the only man I've ever loved doesn't feel the same way about me."

"Unrequited love sucks," he said bluntly.

"It sure does," she agreed.

He parked behind her SUV and walked her to the front door. As he'd been driving her home, it had started to snow again—thick, fluffy flakes that seemed to dance and twirl in the sky, adding a decidedly romantic touch to the end of the evening.

She stopped at the front door and held her breath, waiting for him to say good-night, wondering if he would try to kiss her—and if she would let him.

"I had a really nice time tonight," he told her.

"Me, too," she said.

Then he leaned down and touched his lips to her cheek. And it was a perfectly nice kiss, but there was absolutely no zing or zip.

She looked into his eyes, and saw her own disappointment reflected there.

"We're never going to fall in love, are we?" she asked regretfully.

He shook his head. "I don't think so. But that doesn't mean we can't hang out sometimes to help keep the gossip mill churnin'—because I'd much rather people speculate on what we're doin' together than feel sorry for us because we're two singles in a town where everyone else seems to be pairin' up."

"I would, too," she agreed.

He followed her home.

As Jamie sat in his truck, pulled over to the side of the road with his headlights turned off, and squinted through the window toward the distant and dimly lit front porch of the O'Reilly residence, he realized he'd officially crossed the line from friend to stalker.

He wasn't proud of himself, but he couldn't make himself pull away, either. Not until he knew that her date had gone.

He'd thought he was okay with Fallon going out with Bobby Ray Ellis. Truthfully, he had no right or reason to object to her going out with anyone. But what he'd realized when he saw her at the high school with Bobby Ray, the other man's arm draped across the back of her chair while the movie played on the screen in front of them, was that while the idea of Fallon being on a date didn't bother him, the reality had a very different effect.

And when he realized he'd pulled out of the parking lot behind Bobby Ray's truck after the movie was over, he decided that he would follow her home, just to be sure that she made it there safely. Except that Bobby Ray's truck had unexpectedly pulled into an empty spot by Daisy's Donuts.

Of course, Jamie had no intention of sitting in his truck and waiting for them to come out again. But somehow, that's exactly what happened. For almost forty minutes, while Fallon and Bobby Ray were cozied up together drinking coffee or hot chocolate or whatever, he'd sat in his truck and waited, periodically idling his engine so he didn't freeze his butt to the leather seat.

And then, when they finally left Daisy's Donuts, he'd followed Bobby Ray's truck to the O'Reilly property to ensure the man was taking Fallon home. Of course, from his position on the road, he couldn't see what they were doing or hear what they were talking about. He could only tell that they stood close together on the porch for three minutes, which wasn't a very long time but not a quick good-night, either.

Only when he saw Bobby Ray's truck pull away in the swirling snow did he call it a night.

He made a point of being gone before Fallon showed up Monday morning, and he stayed away until his grumbling stomach insisted that it was time for lunch. He got back to the house just as she was grilling cheese sandwiches for the kids. She buttered four more slices of bread and dropped his sandwiches into the hot pan while she cut the others into bite-size pieces.

"So…did you and Bobby Ray have a good time at the movie the other night?" Jamie finally asked her.

"Yes, we did," she said. "Did you?"

"It was good to get away from the ranch for a while," he said, because that was true. But he didn't remember anything about the movie despite the fact that he'd seen it at least a dozen times before. He couldn't keep his focus on the screen because his gaze kept slipping to the back of Fallon's chair and the other man's arm draped across it.

He had nothing against Bobby Ray. He'd known the guy casually for a lot of years and generally liked him well enough. But he didn't like the idea of him touching Fallon. Or kissing Fallon. And he couldn't bear to consider the possibility of anything more than that.

He knew his feelings were both irrational and unreasonable. But she wasn't just his friend, she was his best friend, and if she and Bobby Ray became a couple, she would spend more time with the other man and less time with him. Okay, so he was irrational, unreasonable *and* selfish.

He knew that Fallon wanted to get married and have a family of her own, and if anyone was meant to be a wife and a mother, it was Fallon. She was so warm and kind and giving—the type of woman he should have married.

He helped himself to a mug of coffee, surreptitiously watching her while she flipped his sandwiches. He'd noticed that she was dressing differently these days. Instead of her usual plaid flannel shirts, she was wearing more fitted styles in more feminine colors.

The top she was wearing today was cream-colored, with tucks at the side that helped it mold to her shape and dozens of tiny hooks down the front to hold the two sides together but made him think how easy it might be to spread them apart. Her jeans looked new, also, and hugged her shapely curves a little more closely than he was accustomed to. She was decorating herself with jewelry, too—sparkly stones in her ears and jangly bracelets on her wrists.

"When is your hair going to go back to normal?"

She blinked at the abrupt question as she plated his sandwiches. "What?"

"You curls are gone," he said.

"They're not actually gone," she admitted. "I've just been straightening my hair."

"Why?"

"Because I wanted a change."

"Why?" he asked again, sincerely baffled by her decision.

"Do I need a reason?"

"Well, generally if something isn't broke, you don't fix it," he said.

She frowned at the irritation in his tone. "How does that apply to my hair?"

"It was just fine the way it was."

"Just fine," she echoed.

"The other way suited you."

"And this doesn't suit me?"

He looked at her again. "I guess it looks okay," he relented. "It just doesn't look like you."

"Bobby Ray seems to like it," she told him.

"So are you like dating him now?"

"We've had one date," she pointed out. "I don't think either one of us is in a hurry to put a label on our relationship."

He scowled. "What does that even mean?"

"It means that my relationship with him is none of your business," she told him.

"Is it wrong for a friend to express concern?"

"No," she acknowledged. "But there's no reason for you to be concerned."

"He hasn't dated anyone exclusively since he broke up with Jillian."

"So?"

"So I just don't want you to get hung up on a guy who's still hung up on someone else," he said.

"Yeah, falling for a guy who isn't capable of reciprocating my feelings would be a stupid move on my part, wouldn't it?" she noted dryly.

"I'm not saying he's not a good guy. I'm just saying that you should be careful."

"Maybe I'm tired of being careful."

He scowled. "What kind of a statement is that?"

"An honest one," she told him. "All my life, I've been a good girl. A good daughter. A good student. A good friend. I've followed the rules without question or complaint, accepting what was offered to me instead of going after what I wanted."

"And Bobby Ray is what you want?"

Her response wasn't at all what he'd expected. Instead of a yes or a no, she took a step closer to him, then lifted herself up onto her toes and kissed him.

Shock held him immobile for about two seconds, then the soft seduction of her lips penetrated the haze that enveloped his brain. Heat pulsed through his system, and he forgot all of the reasons that this was a bad idea and kissed her back.

Just one taste, he promised himself. But her lips were warm and sweet, and one taste wasn't enough. His hands were clenched at his sides, because he knew that if he touched her now, he wouldn't be able to stop. But he really wanted to touch her.

While his head warred with his hormones, she eased her mouth from his and stepped back.

"What was that?" he asked, when enough brain func

tion had been restored that he was able to put words together and form the question.

She ran the tip of her tongue slowly over her bottom lip, as if savoring his flavor. "A test," she said lightly.

His brows rose. "Did I pass?"

Her mouth turned up, just a little at the corners. "I haven't decided yet if I'm grading on a curve."

"Grading on a curve?" he echoed, torn between insult and amusement. "In that case, I want a redo."

But she turned away from him to grab her coat off of the hook by the door. "I have to go."

"You can't just kiss a guy like that and walk away," he protested.

"Watch me," she said.

He stood there, stunned and aroused, and did just that.

Chapter Eleven

"I thought you were going to make my brother do this," Bella said to Fallon, as they stood in line with the babies at the center court of the mall Wednesday afternoon, waiting for their turn to see Santa.

"That was the plan, but Jamie's been so busy with the ranch…and now with Andy and Molly, too," she said, referring to the puppies by the names he'd given them—names apparently inspired by the characters in one of Bella's favorite childhood movies.

"He didn't have to bring those puppies home," his sister pointed out.

Fallon slid her friend a look. "Really? Knowing your brother as well as you do, you can actually say that with a straight face?"

"You're right," Bella acknowledged. "I guess I should be proud of the fact that he only kept two of the seven."

Fallon inched forward with the stroller as two more kids scrambled toward the sleigh, eager to share their Christmas wishes with jolly old St. Nick. She was impressed with his appearance and demeanor. If his beard was fake, it certainly didn't look it. And he seemed incredibly patient with all of the kids—even the screaming babies and toddlers. And there had been a lot of screamers.

Thankfully, HJK didn't seem to be bothered by the other kids' crying. Maybe because, in the first few months, one or more of them had always been in tears, so they'd learned not to be swayed by the others' emotions.

They inched forward in the line again. Fallon reached down and unfurled Katie's fingers from the hem of her dress and pulled the skirt away from her mouth, swapping it for a pacifier. Since she'd started teething, she would chew on anything and everything she could get her hands on.

Behind Katie, Jared was trying to take his shoes off his feet, playing with the laces and knots. Henry was happy just to watch the people go by. He was, of the three babies, the most content and easy to please. Jared was a little more high energy and Katie was downright demanding at times, but Fallon loved the individual personality of each of them.

When it was finally their turn to see Santa, Katie balked for a moment when she heard the booming "Ho Ho Ho," but Bella and Fallon coaxed her into overcoming her apprehension and letting herself be perched on Santa's knee.

It took half a dozen attempts to get a picture with all three kids looking at least in the general vicinity of the camera, and Fallon would have been happy with that—as would the dozens of parents waiting in line behind them. But Santa seemed content to chat with the kids while the photographer kept snapping away. It was probably more by luck than design that he did end up with a picture in which Henry, Jared and Katie were all looking into the camera and smiling—and which Fallon decided would be a perfect Christmas present for their daddy.

"Aside from putting up a tree, has my brother complied with any of the other requests on your holiday cheer list?" Bella asked, as they made their way through the mall.

"Well, he hasn't objected to listening to the Christmas music I usually have on."

"I don't think the absence of an objection earns a check mark," Bella said dryly.

"He's been eating the Christmas cookies I've baked."

"Okay, he gets points for bravery."

Fallon narrowed her gaze on her friend.

"I'm kidding. I'm sure they were…edible."

"They were delicious," she insisted.

"But he didn't help you make them and he didn't eat them because they were shaped like bells or wreaths," Bella pointed out. "He ate them because they were cookies."

"Still…baby steps," Fallon said.

"Any luck convincing him to attend the Candlelight Walk?"

"Not yet," she admitted.

"I can't figure out if you're incredibly patient or extremely stubborn," Bella said. "But I'm grateful that you're not giving up on him."

Fallon wasn't sure of her motivation, either. The only thing she knew for certain was that giving up on Jamie had never been an option.

When Jamie walked into the house at the end of a very long day on Wednesday, he discovered that Fallon was wearing one of those skirts again. The short kind that showed off a mile of leg between the bottom of the hem and the top of her boots. Her sweater had a modest neckline and long sleeves, but it hugged her torso like a lover's hands.

He tore his gaze away from her tempting feminine curves and focused his attention on his babies, giving them lots of love and cuddles because coming home to them was always his favorite part of the day. Of course, the puppies wanted their share of attention, too, so he scratched their ears and rubbed their bellies.

"There's a lasagna in the oven for your dinner," Fallon said. "It should be ready in half an hour."

He nodded. "Thanks." And though he didn't intend to say anything else, the next words spilled out of his mouth of their own volition. "Why are you dressed like that?"

"I'm going for dinner with Bobby Ray," she told him.

"Where are you going?"

"Just over to the Ace."

He scowled. "You can't go to the Ace dressed like that."

"I'm twenty-four years old," she reminded him. "I don't even let my mother tell me what to wear anymore."

"Do you want to start a brawl?"

"I'm hardly the type of woman who inspires that kind of behavior," she retorted.

"You're a woman," he said. "Sometimes that's the only inspiration a drunk cowboy needs."

"Thank you for that incredibly flattering assessment," she said dryly.

The furrow in his brow deepened. "You don't need me to tell you that you're an attractive woman."

"Maybe I do."

"Well, you are," he said. "You should be able to see that for yourself every time you look in the mirror."

Her lips curved. "Do you really think so?"

"Geez, Fallon, you're not actually hoping to stir up trouble, are you?"

"Maybe I am," she said. "Maybe I'm tired of every man I know treating me like a buddy. Maybe I want someone to look at me and realize I'm a woman, to want me as a woman."

And suddenly he got it. "You mean me," he realized. "You want *me* to see you as a woman."

She sighed as she shook her head. "No. I think I've finally accepted that that is never going to happen."

"But I do see you as a woman," he assured her. "A genuinely warm, funny and smart woman."

"Maybe it's un-PC," she admitted. "But I don't want to be admired for my personality or my intelligence. I want to be wanted."

He swallowed. "You're looking for a hookup?"

"That wouldn't be my first choice," she said. "But I've decided to open my mind up to any and all possibilities."

"A hookup should not be one of them," he told her. "You deserve better than that."

She walked to the door, then turned back. "What

does the song say—we can't always get what we want, but we get what we need?"

"Don't go, Fallon." The words were out of his mouth before he realized what he was saying.

She paused with her hand on the doorknob.

"Don't go out with Bobby Ray tonight."

She slowly turned around, her expression carefully neutral. "Are you making me an alternate offer?" she asked.

He nodded. "Stay here. With me."

She held his gaze for a moment, considering his invitation. "What would we do?"

His mind immediately filled with possible answers to her question, none of which she'd go home and tell her mother about. And while he wasn't just ready but eager to explore each and every one of those possibilities, he realized that he needed to be smart—to think about what would happen after and the potential consequences to their relationship. Getting personally involved with Fallon was a risk he couldn't take.

"Forget I said anything," he decided. "Go out with Bobby Ray tonight."

Fallon shook her head. "You flip-flop more than a fish out of water."

"I'm sorry," he said, and meant it. "I'm trying to be smart here and your friendship is too important to me to risk jeopardizing it."

"Forget about being smart and tell me, honestly, what you want."

"I want you to stay," he admitted. "I want…you."

She pulled her cell phone out of her pocket, tapped her fingers over the keypad, then tucked the phone away again. "I'll stay."

* * *

Jamie opened a bottle of wine to go with the lasagna they had for dinner. After they'd finished eating, they cleaned up the kitchen and spent some time playing with the babies. It was all part of a routine that she'd performed with him countless times before. But tonight, after Henry, Jared and Katie had been bathed and changed and were asleep in their cribs, Fallon wasn't getting ready to leave.

Jamie poured some more wine into her glass, and her hand shook as she lifted it to her lips.

"You're nervous," he noted.

"A little," she admitted.

"Have you changed your mind?"

She shook her head. "No, but I can't help thinking about how this is going to change our relationship," she confided.

"Change isn't always a bad thing," he said, taking the wine glass from her hand and setting it down on the counter beside his. Then he put his arms around her and drew her toward him.

Now, she thought. Finally now he would kiss her and she could stop thinking about what was going to happen and enjoy the experience of letting it happen.

But he bypassed her mouth in favor of her temple, gently skimming his lips over her skin. Then he brushed a kiss on her cheekbone, another near her ear, and her jaw. He wasn't kissing her so much as caressing her face with his lips, and every fleeting touch was incredibly and shockingly arousing.

His hands slid beneath her sweater, his fingertips danced over her skin. He was a rancher with big hands and tough skin, but his touch was infinitely and almost unbearably gentle. No, he wasn't touching so much as teasing, hinting at the promise of so much more.

His hands moved around to her front, stroking gently over her belly, tracing the edge of her bra. He hadn't touched her breasts, but her nipples were already peaked, aching.

"Are you trying to drive me crazy?"

"Is it working?"

"Yes."

He smiled. "I like the feel of your skin." Then he nuzzled her throat. "The scent of your skin." Then he pressed his lips to the ultra sensitive spot where her neck met her shoulder. "And the taste of your skin."

"You could touch, smell and taste a lot more if you took me upstairs to your bedroom," she told him.

Jamie didn't need to be told twice.

Upstairs, he pulled back the covers on his bed, then laid her down on the mattress.

It had been a long time since he'd been with a woman. He didn't remember exactly how long, except that the last time Paula had let him touch her had been in the early stages of her pregnancy, before she discovered she was carrying triplets.

He pushed those unhappy memories aside to focus on the joy that filled his heart here and now.

Fallon was passionate and eager, responding to his kisses, his touches, with wild abandon, meeting his demands with her own. He knew she was self-conscious about what she considered to be her too-small breasts, but to him they were perfect. Round and firm with dark pink nipples at the center.

He took one of those nipples in his mouth, then the other. She squirmed beneath him as he suckled her flesh, her breath coming in short, shallow gasps that assured him she was enjoying the attention. He proceeded to pay the same careful attention to the rest of her body. He moved slowly down her torso, his mouth trailing kisses over her silky skin.

He slid his hands along the inside of her thighs, urging them apart. Then he parted the soft folds at her center, to reveal her sweet glistening core. She sucked in a breath, her fingers curling into the sheet. He interpreted her silence as acquiescence and lowered his head to taste her.

Her heels dug into the mattress, her hips instinctively tilting to provide easier access. He took advantage of what she was offering, using his lips and his tongue to give them both pleasure.

"Jamie. Please." She was writhing beneath him, gasping for breath. He knew what she was asking for, because he wanted the same thing. He was rock-hard and aching, desperate for her.

He shifted away from her only long enough to dig a little square packet out of the drawer in his night table, then huffed out a frustrated breath.

"What's wrong?" Fallon asked.

"It's been a long time since I've had any need for birth control, and I'm pretty sure this condom is past its best before date," he admitted.

"Oh," she said, the single syllable heavy with disappointment.

"I don't suppose you have any in your purse?" he asked hopefully.

"No, I—wait. Actually, I do," she admitted, and even in the dim light, he could see her cheeks flush. "But they're, uh, glow-in-the-dark condoms."

"Aren't you full of surprises?" he teased.

"I'm not. I mean, they're not mine." She lifted her hands to cover her face. "Brenna tucked them in my purse, as a joke, before I went out with Bobby Ray Saturday night."

He absolutely was not going to ask if she'd used any of the condoms, because he definitely did not want to know. "If you could not talk about other men while you're naked in my bed, that would be great," he suggested.

Her next words ignored his advice and rekindled his ardor.

"I didn't sleep with Bobby Ray," she told him. "I wouldn't be here with you if I had."

He brushed a quick kiss on her lips. "Where's your purse?"

"In the kitchen."

"I'll be right back," he promised. Then he slid from the bed, quickly wrapped himself in his robe and took the stairs two at a time.

He was gone less than a minute. When he handed her the purse, she unzipped the side pouch of her purse and pulled out a handful of condoms.

He took one and set the others on top of the night table, then tore open the package and quickly sheathed himself.

"Wow," Fallon commented. "It really does glow."

"Give me a minute," he said. "And you'll be saying 'wow' for a different reason."

Her lips curved as she reached for him, her hands eagerly exploring his body, sliding over his chest, his shoulders and down his back.

The muscles in his arms quivered with the effort of

holding himself over her as he fought against the primitive instinct to drive into her, hard and deep. Instead he slowly eased into her. Despite her obvious arousal, his entry wasn't easy. She was tighter than he'd expected, and he could feel the tension in her body as she braced herself to take him.

He was a little tense, too, trying not to think about the fact they were passing the point of no return. Then he kissed her again, slowly and deeply until he felt some of the tension leave her body, and he eased in a little deeper.

He was trying to hold onto his patience, to show some restraint, but Fallon apparently decided that she was having none of that. She lifted her legs to hook them at his back and tilted her hips to pull him deeper, gasping with shock as he finally pushed through a barrier he hadn't expected to encounter.

He froze, as shocked disbelief penetrated the euphoria of his arousal.

"You were a virgin," he realized.

"Can we save the talking for later?" she suggested.

His fingers curled into the comforter, and he gripped the fabric tightly in his fists. "I think we need to talk about this."

But she shook her head. "Not now. Please, Jamie. I've waited too long for this—for *you*—to stop now."

Then, just in case the words weren't sufficient to make him lose the tenuous grip on his self-control, she started to move her hips again. Whatever she lacked in experience, she more than made up for with enthusiasm, and he finally gave himself over to the passion that consumed them both.

* * *

Fallon had dreamed of making love with Jamie, but even her most vivid and erotic dreams did not compare to the reality. Even without knowing he was her first, he'd been a careful and attentive lover, ensuring her pleasure before taking his own. She exhaled a contented sigh, though she knew the blissful peace of the moment wouldn't last.

Jamie would have questions, and he'd demand answers, and though the last thing she wanted to do was dissect the most amazing experience of her life, she understood that she at least owed him an explanation.

"You should have told me," he said.

"I figured you already had enough reasons for not wanting to get naked with me without adding any more to the list."

"I don't know that I would have been able to stop myself from making love with you," he admitted. "But I do know I would have been more careful."

She stroked a hand down his back, because now that she'd finally had the opportunity to touch him, she didn't want to stop. "You didn't hurt me, Jamie."

"Are you sure?"

"I realize that I'm the inexperienced one here, but I would have figured the fact that I climaxed a few times and bit down on your shoulder so that I didn't shout would be clues that I had a pretty good time."

His lips curved. "A pretty good time, huh?"

"But maybe I should be asking how it was for you," she realized.

"It was amazing. *You* were amazing."

"Of course, it has been fifteen months since you've had sex," she reminded him.

He brushed his lips against hers, softly, sweetly.

"You were amazing," he said again.

But she could tell by the slight furrow in his brow that he was still worried about something, and she had a pretty good idea about the cause of his concern.

"I wasn't saving myself for anyone—or for any particular reason," she told him, unwilling to admit—even to herself—that she had done exactly that. "So please don't make this into something bigger than it is."

"It is pretty big," he told her.

"Now you're just bragging," she admonished.

It took him a second, then he chuckled softly. "You really are full of surprises, aren't you, Fallon O'Reilly?"

"In a good way, I hope."

He brushed his lips over hers. "The very best way."

When Jamie slid out of bed a short while later to check on the kids and let the puppies outside, Fallon decided to sneak into his shower. She wasn't embarrassed by or ashamed of what had happened between them, but she didn't want to advertise it, either. She turned on the faucet and adjusted the temperature, then stepped beneath the spray.

She had just lathered up a washcloth with soap when the curtain was yanked back, making her yelp.

"What are you doing?" she demanded, when Jamie stepped into the shower with her.

"I'm a conservationist and I'm saving water."

She instinctively crossed her arms over her body.

Jamie chuckled. "Have you forgotten that I've already seen every inch of your body?"

"Not under bright lights," she argued.

"A definite oversight," he said, wrapping his fingers around her wrists and pulling her hands away.

"You are so beautiful, Fallon. So perfect."

"I'm not even close to being perfect," she denied.

"A wise woman once told me that perfect doesn't have to mean without flaws but only what fulfills your need in the moment."

"Didn't I already fulfill your need?"

He smiled as he slid his hands up her back. "Yeah, but I need you again."

"Do you now?"

"I have a feeling that you could become an addiction," he told her.

She wanted to believe he was telling her the truth, that his desire for her could be even half as deep and real as her need for him. At the same time, she was trying to tread carefully. Because while the physical aspect of their relationship was new territory, she'd accepted her feelings for him a long time ago.

She was still trying to decide on an appropriate response when he lathered up his hands and began to spread the soap over her body, effectively scrubbing all rational thoughts from her brain.

"What are you doing?" she asked instead.

"Showing you there are more benefits to sharing a shower than just saving water."

He nudged her under the spray, to wash away the suds, then dipped his head to touch his lips to the cluster of freckles on her shoulder, then trailed his mouth across her collarbone. "Your skin is so soft."

"Your body is so hard," she noted, letting her hands explore the rugged contours of his shoulders, his pecs, his abs. And lower. She boldly wrapped her fingers around the rigid length of him. "All over."

He slapped a hand against the shower wall behind her and closed his eyes. "You're a fast learner, aren't you?"

"Actually, I think I'm a pretty slow learner. In fact, we're probably going to have to practice over and over again before I really figure this out."

"Over and over again?"

"Over—" she stroked him again, slowly, from base to tip, and back again "—and over."

A long time later, after they'd made love again—this time in the bed—and his heart rate had finally slowed to something approximating normal, Jamie wrapped a strand of damp hair around his finger and tugged gently. "There they are."

She blinked slowly, as if trying to bring the world back into focus. "What?"

He smiled, gratified to know that he'd rocked her world as completely as she'd rocked his. "Your curls," he said. "I thought they were gone forever."

"I wish."

"I don't. I like your curls."

She seemed surprised by that admission. "You do?"

He nodded. "And as much as I like the way you look in a short skirt, you're every bit as appealing in a pair of jeans."

She made a sound of disbelief. "You never looked at me twice until I started wearing skirts," she pointed out to him.

"I always looked," he told her. "I just never let you see me looking."

"Why?"

"Because I was afraid that if I tried to turn our friendship into something more and it didn't work out, I'd lose my best friend."

"And now?"

He tucked a strand of hair behind her ear. "I'm still worried," he admitted. "I don't ever want to lose you, Fallon."

"You won't lose me," she told him. "But I do have to leave your bed right now."

"Why?"

"Because it's late and we both have to get up early."

"It's not that late," he said, though she could tell he was having trouble keeping his eyes open.

"And your sister's going to be home soon."

"Maybe," he acknowledged.

"Do you really want to explain this—" she gestured between the two of them "—to Bella?"

"Not tonight," he admitted.

She brushed her lips to his. "And that's why I need to go."

He slid a hand up her thigh to settle at the curve of her butt. "Are you here tomorrow?"

"Ten months," she said, shaking her head. "And you still don't know the schedule."

"The schedule keeps changing," he said in his defense.

"I've always done Monday and Thursday mornings, full days on Wednesdays and the occasional Saturday."

"So I'll see you in the morning?"

"Yes, you'll see me in the morning," she assured him.

"Good." He framed her face in his hands and brought his mouth down to hers, kissing her softly, deeply.

"And if you want to see me the following night, you

could give me a call and ask me to go to the Candlelight Walk with you, Henry, Jared and Katie," she suggested.

"You're determined to drag us out to that, aren't you?"

She shrugged. "It's just an idea, but I know that's where I'm going to be Friday night."

"I'll give you a call," he promised.

Chapter Twelve

She was twenty-four years old and sneaking into her house as if she were a teenager out past curfew.

Fallon had no experience with that kind of subversive behavior. As a teenager, she'd never broken curfew. She'd always been a good girl, a rule follower. Tonight, she'd broken a lot of rules, and she couldn't deny that it felt pretty darn good.

How many times had she sat in the high school cafeteria listening to her friends and classmates recount and evaluate their sexual experiences, without having anything to add to the conversation? Truthfully, she'd always suspected that sex was overhyped. She knew better now.

Tonight, she'd made love with the man she loved, and the experience had surpassed every one of her expectations.

The only tiny niggling concern was that she didn't know how Jamie felt about her. Suggesting that he might become addicted to her was the closest he'd come to any kind of emotional declaration, and that was okay. She understood that men didn't engage their emotions as readily as women did. She also understood that he might still be grieving the loss of his wife. Maybe he was even still in love with his wife.

That possibility took a little bit of the spring from her step. She'd never believed that Paula deserved him, but she'd supported his choices because he was her friend, because she loved him and wanted him to be happy. She'd sincerely hoped that Paula would make him happy, and she had—for a while. But Fallon knew there had been issues and tensions in their marriage—as there were in any marriage—and Paula had died before they could be resolved, one way or another.

As a result, it wouldn't surprise her to learn that Jamie had some lingering feelings for his wife—the mother of his children. She only hoped those feelings wouldn't prevent him from letting himself fall in love and be loved again.

She was tiptoeing toward the stairs when she heard the scrabbling sound of paws and a trio of excited yips from Duchess—the puppy her parents had chosen from Andy and Molly's littermates.

"Shh," she admonished, crouching to scratch behind the pup's ears.

Duchess dropped to the ground then rolled onto her back, a not-so-subtle demand for Fallon to rub her belly—which she did, because she knew it would keep her quiet.

After she'd fussed over the animal for a few minutes, she pointed toward the kitchen. "Now go back to bed."

Surprisingly, the dog obeyed her command and Fallon headed up the stairs. At the top, she turned automatically toward her bedroom—and nearly bumped into Brenna, who had just stepped out of the bathroom.

Her sister blinked, as if trying to focus in the darkness. "Fallon?"

"Hey, Brenna," she whispered softly.

"What time is it?"

"Late," she hedged.

"Obviously." Brenna grabbed her arm and steered her into her bedroom, where she glanced at the clock on her bedside table. "It's almost three a.m."

"Early rather than late then," she said lightly.

Brenna pushed her toward the bed. "Sit."

And though she wasn't a child and her sister had no right to boss her around or interrogate her, she sat.

Brenna perched on the edge of her desk chair, facing Fallon. "Now spill."

"Can't this wait until morning?"

"As you pointed out, it is morning."

Fallon sighed. "Come on, Bren—I just want to catch a few hours' sleep before I have to get up."

"This conversation can be long or short, depending on how willing you are to answer my questions," her sister said.

"You're not my mother, so don't try to act like you are."

"Would you like me to wake Mom up so you can have this conversation with her instead?" Brenna challenged.

She sighed. "No."

"Where were you?" her sister prompted.

"I was at The Short Hills Ranch," she admitted.

"With Bella?"

She lifted her chin to meet her sister's gaze. "With Jamie."

To her surprise, Brenna smiled. "So maybe he's not as much of a clueless idiot as I was beginning to think."

Fallon just stared at her.

"Did you think I would judge you for being with the man you've loved for most of your life?" her sister asked softly.

"Is there anyone who doesn't know how I feel about him?"

"Probably Jamie," Fiona said, as she slipped into the room and sat on the edge of the bed beside her youngest sister. "Men can be so oblivious about certain things."

"She's right about that," Brenna confirmed.

"Did we wake you up?" Fallon asked, worriedly.

"No, I was awake," Fiona assured her.

"Maybe our big sister has a man on her mind, too," Brenna teased.

Fiona's only response was a shake of her head—whether a denial or an indication that she didn't want to talk about it, Fallon never had a chance to ask before Fiona spoke again. "Are you okay?" she asked gently. "Were you careful?"

"Yes and yes," she said, more touched than embarrassed by her older sisters' questions and concern.

"Good." Fiona kissed her cheek. "Now go to sleep so the rest of us can, too."

The Candlelight Walk was exactly that—a leisurely stroll from one end of Main Street to the other, undertaken by residents carrying lighted candles and singing along with the Christmas music that accompanied their journey. At the end of the processional, there was a big bonfire and refreshments were served.

The first Christmas after their wedding, Jamie and Paula had attended the event, and Paula had griped that it was cold. Even with two sets of mittens, she'd complained that her hands were icy. The second year, they'd skipped the event entirely. And last year, they'd barely been on speaking terms.

Which was probably why he'd resisted Fallon's efforts to embrace the holidays—because all of his memories from the previous year had been unhappy ones. But she'd refused to let his "bah, humbug" attitude dampen her own holiday spirit. She'd surrounded him with all the sights and sounds and scents of Christmas—not just the tree in his living room but decorations around the house, holiday music pumping out of her iPod, the scent of gingerbread baking (and though he had initially been wary, the cookies had been really tasty). And now, with Christmas less than two weeks away, he found that he was sincerely looking forward to celebrating the holiday—his first with Henry, Jared and Katie. And hopefully his first with Fallon, too.

But venturing into town and celebrating with all the residents of Rust Creek Falls? He wasn't sure he was quite ready for that.

"Are you sure it's not too cold out for HJK?" he asked worriedly.

"They're wearing three layers beneath their snowsuits," she pointed out to him. "Plus hats on their heads and mittens on their hands. They'll be fine."

"Katie's nose was running this morning."

"Because she's teething."

"I'm not sure about this," he said. "It wasn't so long ago that there was an RSV outbreak in town, and the immune systems of preemies are more fragile than other babies'."

"Why don't you tell me what's really going on here?"

"What do you mean?" he hedged.

"Why don't you like taking your kids into town?" she asked.

"My reluctance isn't really about the kids," he admitted.

She considered his response for a moment before hesitantly asking, "Is it that you don't want to be seen with me?"

"What? No," he responded immediately, eager to dispel her concern. "It's not about you, either."

"Then what is it about?" she pressed.

"The way people look at me," he finally acknowledged. "The sympathy and the pity."

"The respect and admiration," she interjected.

He raised a brow.

"Do you really not see that?" she asked him. "Everyone in town knows how hard you're working to provide for your family, and they respect you for it."

"Not everyone thinks I made the right choices," Jamie told her. "The first time I saw Gramps in town after the babies were born, he told me that they'd be better off in a home with two parents."

She touched a hand to his arm. "I'm sorry—but you have to realize his opinion isn't a popular one."

He nodded. "And when I got over being angry and hurt, I wondered if he was trying to explain to me why they sent Dana and Liza away—because they believed it would be better for them."

"Maybe," she said dubiously. "But then why didn't they find a better option for you and Bella?"

He shrugged. "Maybe because we were too old to appeal to adoptive parents and too young to be left to our own devices."

Whatever the reason, he and his sister had been caught in the middle, living with grandparents who didn't want them and didn't seem to know how to love them. It was no wonder they'd had trouble opening up their hearts. Of course, when he'd finally done so, he'd ended up with his heart broken.

Still, he was sincerely happy to know that Bella had finally fallen in love. His sister deserved to be happy, and it made him happy to watch her planning her future with Hudson. Even if it didn't make him eager to open up his own again. No, thanks—been there, done that, bought the ill-fitting T-shirt and not going back again.

"I could go for a hot chocolate," Fallon said to Jamie, when they'd come to the end of the processional and the crowd had begun to disperse.

"If you want to stay here with HJK, I'll brave the line at the refreshment table to see if there's anything left."

"Thanks."

"Whipped cream or marshmallows?"

"Are you asking what I want in my hot chocolate or is this a question for later?" she teased.

"I was asking about the hot chocolate, but now you've got me wondering," he admitted.

"Marshmallows…for now," she told him.

"And later?"

She smiled. "Whatever you want."

* * *

She went back to Jamie's house for a few hours after the Candlelight Walk, where he made love to her slowly, thoroughly and quietly.

Afterward, he fell asleep with her in his arms, feeling—for the first time in a long time—both happy and optimistic about the future.

He didn't often dream. Or maybe it was more accurate to say that he didn't often remember what he dreamed. But when he woke up in the night, his heart hammering against his ribs, his breath shallow and ragged, the dream was still vivid in his mind.

Not a dream—a nightmare.

He sat up and scrubbed his hands over his face, trying to reassure himself that it was only a dream. That none of it was real.

But it had felt real.

He'd heard Paula's voice as clearly as if she'd been right beside him, telling him that she hadn't really died in the hospital but only pretended to so that she could escape from him and a marriage she'd never really wanted. And now that she'd had some time to think about it and had seen their sweet, beautiful babies, she'd decided that she wanted them after all.

When he told her that she couldn't have them, she just laughed. But she did turn to walk away, and he exhaled a sigh of relief as he watched her go. Until he noticed that Henry, Jared and Katie were following her.

He tried to go after them, but his feet were stuck to the ground. He tried to reach for them, to pull them back, but no matter how far he stretched his arms, it wasn't far enough. He couldn't get to them and they continued to move away, following Paula until they all disappeared into the mist.

Then he heard a sound from another direction and turned to find himself face-to-face with Fallon. She smiled at him sweetly and kissed him softly, then told him she was going to check on their babies. And he had to tell her that they were gone.

She hadn't understood at first. His voice was hoarse and broken and the words didn't make any sense to her. They didn't make any sense to him, either. He didn't want to believe that they were true. But somehow he could see through the window as she hurried into the house and raced up the stairs and into the babies' room. She'd stared at the empty cribs, tears sliding down her cheeks.

"How could you let them go?" she demanded.

He tried to explain. "I didn't let them go, but I couldn't stop them."

"You had only one task—to keep your family together and safe. And you failed. You failed, Jamie."

"I'm sorry."

She shook her head. "Being sorry doesn't change anything."

And then she turned and walked away, following the same path as his ex-wife and his babies, disappearing into the same mist.

Jamie shuddered. It had felt so real, so terrifyingly real. But it was only a dream. A nightmare.

He sucked in a deep breath, then exhaled slowly, attempting to reassure himself that none of it was true.

Except that Fallon was gone.

He'd fallen asleep with her in his arms, and when he'd awakened, she wasn't there.

Logically, he understood that she couldn't stay with him through the night. But he wasn't feeling logical right now. He was feeling alone and abandoned, because she'd left him—just like everyone else he'd ever loved.

Loved?

Now his heart was pounding for a different reason. No, it couldn't be true. It was too soon. Wasn't it?

He'd only been in love once before. He'd fallen fast and hard for Paula, and he'd felt so lucky that she'd fallen for him, too. And look how that had turned out.

He didn't regret the years they'd spent together. How could he when she'd given him Henry, Jared and Katie? But loving and losing Paula had changed him. And though he knew that Fallon wasn't anything like his former wife, he wasn't the same man anymore, either.

He wasn't eager to toss the dice and gamble that this time love would endure. This time, he had too much to lose.

Chapter Thirteen

Fallon had hated leaving the comfort of Jamie's arms and the warmth of his bed, but she knew that any concerns Maureen O'Reilly had about her youngest daughter's relationship with the single father would not be alleviated by her staying out all night. So she'd slipped out of his bed in the early hours of the morning, drove home in the darkness, and slid under the covers of her cold, empty bed, already counting the hours until she would see him again.

Only six more hours, she promised herself, and drifted off to sleep with a smile on her face.

It was a relatively short period of time, but when Fallon walked in the back door of Jamie's house six hours later, she instinctively sensed that something had changed.

Or maybe it was just that the house was unusually

quiet, the three high chairs in the kitchen empty and no sign of Henry, Jared or Katie anywhere around. Only Jamie was there, sitting at the table with a mug of coffee in his hands and a grim expression on his face.

"Where are the kids?" she asked.

"Bella and Hudson offered to take them for a few hours this morning."

"Oh." It was a perfectly reasonable explanation, but there were too many things that didn't add up. They'd made love just last night...they were alone in the house...and he hadn't even kissed her.

"What aren't you telling me?" she finally asked him.

He refilled his mug with coffee, then set it down again without drinking. "I don't know how to say it," he began.

Her heart did a freefall into the bottom of her stomach. "You're breaking up with me," she realized.

"No," he denied, though not very convincingly. "I'm just suggesting that we...take a step back."

"A step back," she echoed hollowly. "What, exactly, is that supposed to mean?"

"Everything happened so fast. I just think we should take some time to think about what we really want from one another."

Fast? She almost laughed. Only if seven years after their first kiss was fast.

But maybe, from his perspective, it was fast. His wife—the mother of his babies—had died only ten months earlier. Maybe it wasn't unreasonable for him to need some more time to adjust to the changes in their relationship.

"How much time?" she asked, her tone carefully neutral. "A few days? A couple of weeks?"

He didn't meet her gaze. "I don't know."

She suddenly felt hollow and empty inside, drained of all happiness and hope. "Do you really want time— or are you trying to get out of a situation you wish you'd never gotten into?"

"I don't regret being with you, Fallon."

"But you don't want to be with me anymore," she guessed.

"I don't want to lose my best friend," he told her.

She nodded. "That's always a good one—hard to argue against."

"It's true," he insisted. "You are one of few people in my life that I know I can count on."

"And, somehow, sharing your bed makes me unreliable?"

"You're determined to make this difficult, aren't you?"

"Forgive me," she said. "I've never been dumped by a lover, so I'm not entirely sure how I'm supposed to react."

"I'm not dumping you," he denied.

"No? Because that's what it feels like from this end."

"You deserve someone who can give you what you want," he told her. "And that's not going to be me."

"How do you know what I want?" she challenged.

"Because I know *you*. Because I know that you've always dreamed of having a husband and a family, and maybe you look at me and the babies and think we're the quickest route to everything you've ever wanted."

"Apparently you don't know me at all," she shot back, her tone practically vibrating with suppressed fury. "Because I don't think of you and the babies as a 'route' to anything, but as the man and the children I love."

He shook his head regretfully. "I'm not a good bet, Fallon."

"Oh, this one I know," she said, still fuming. "The 'it's not you, it's me' speech."

"It's not a speech—it's the truth," he insisted. "I've been married, and it didn't turn out well."

"We slept together a few times," she pointed out to him. "I may be naïve and inexperienced, but I'm not holding my breath for a proposal."

"Maybe not yet," he acknowledged. "But you can't tell me that you weren't hoping our relationship was headed in that direction."

She felt the sting of hot tears behind her eyes, but she refused to let them fall. "You're right. I did think, considering our history of friendship, common interests and goals, that we might have a future together."

"And I can't go down that road again," he said. "I've loved and lost too many people in my life to risk losing you, too."

Too many people.

Those words successfully defused her anger, because she realized now that this wasn't just about their relationship or even the loss of his wife—this went back much further and much deeper. Unfortunately, the words did nothing to staunch the bleeding of her heart.

She understood that he'd been scarred by the loss of his parents, the abandonment by his brothers and the disappearance of his youngest sisters, which was why she'd wanted to help him reunite with his siblings. But any time she'd broached the subject with him, he'd shot it down.

Just as he was shooting down her feelings and her hopes for a future for them together now. "So what do you want—for us to go back to being just friends again?"

"I think that would be for the best," he said.

But it wasn't. Not for her, anyway. She didn't want to be "just friends" with the man she loved—the man she'd always loved. She'd given him all of her heart, and he was handing it back to her like an unwelcome gift.

Tears welled in her eyes again, and she turned away so that he wouldn't see them. "I don't know if that's possible now."

"It is," he insisted. "You just have to be willing."

Was she willing?

She wanted so much more than he was offering, but if all he could give her was friendship, she would take that rather than lose him forever.

"Please, Fallon," he implored.

And because she'd never been able to deny him anything he wanted, she nodded.

But before they could go back to being "just friends," she needed a little bit of time to pick up the pieces of her broken heart. "Okay," she finally responded. "I'm going out of town for a few days, but we can talk when I get back."

He frowned at that. "You're leaving town?"

"Just for a few days," she told him.

"Because of this?"

"No," she denied. "This has been in the works for a while. In fact, I've already talked to Bella to ensure that the baby chain has you covered."

"You're really going to abandon Henry, Jared and Katie," he said, more of a statement than a question.

"I'm not abandoning them," she said gently. "And I'm not abandoning you, either."

Maybe she didn't see it that way, but from where Jamie was standing, it certainly felt as if he was being abandoned.

"When will you be back?" he demanded.

"I'm not sure."

He wanted to ask her not to go, but he knew he had no right. Instead, he asked, "Where are you going?"

She lifted herself onto her toes and touched her lips to his cheek. "I'll see you soon."

Then she turned, and he was left standing there, watching her walk away and wondering if he'd just made the biggest mistake of his life.

When Jamie headed back to the house after completing his morning chores, he found his sister had returned and was sitting at the kitchen table looking at sample wedding invitations while the babies played.

He poured himself a mug of coffee and sat down across from Bella. "Fallon told me that she talked to you about her plans to go out of town."

She nodded. "Since school is on break for the holidays, Paige Traub is going to cover Fallon's usual shifts, which will give the kids a chance to hang out with her son, Carter. And Cecelia Pritchett had to cancel her Thursday afternoon because she's got an appointment in Kalispell, but Margot Crawford can fill in for her. The revised schedule is on the fridge."

He didn't really care about the revised schedule. He wanted to know where Fallon had gone—and when she'd be back. But if he started asking his sister all kinds of questions, she'd figure out that he'd screwed things up with Fallon, and he wasn't prepared to talk about it. Not until he'd figured out how he was going to fix it.

So far, he didn't have any ideas in that direction, and sitting around thinking about the mistakes he'd made would drive him crazy. Instead, he reached for the box of invitations Bella had set aside, deciding that he could distract himself by helping her.

She snatched the box away from him. "Don't you have stables to muck out or something?"

"Already done," he told her.

"Fence to fix?"

"Finished that last week."

"Then you obviously don't need me to hang around here," she said pushing her chair away from the table. "Which is good, because Hudson and I are going in to Kalispell to see about a cake for the wedding."

"Your wedding isn't until June—won't the cake be stale by then?"

"Ha-ha." She kissed his cheek. "Have a good day, big brother."

"Actually, I might head into the city today, too," he decided impulsively.

"For what?" she asked suspiciously.

"To take HJK to the mall."

Bella's brows drew together as she touched the back of her hand to his forehead, as if checking for a fever. "Are you ill?"

He scowled at her. "No, I'm not ill."

"But it's eight days before Christmas—and a Saturday—and you want to take three babies to a shopping mall in the city?"

No, he didn't really *want* to, but he remembered Fallon's repeated urgings for him to have the kids' first Christmas commemorated by a photo with Santa—and his repeated brush-offs.

He lifted a shoulder. "Fallon seemed to think it was important for Henry, Jared and Katie to see Santa, and I thought she might like a picture of them with the big guy."

Bella opened her mouth as if she was going to say something, then apparently changed her mind and closed it again.

"You don't think I can handle an outing with my own children?" he challenged.

"I'm sure you can handle it," she finally said. "But I think you might benefit from an extra set of hands. Why don't I go with you, then Hudson can pick me up at the mall and we'll do our rounds of the bakeries afterward?"

Which was her way of saying that she didn't think he could handle a trip into the city with his own kids. And while his pride urged him to decline her offer, his rational mind reminded him that three babies were a handful on the best of days. "I don't want you to change your plans on my account," he said.

"I'm not changing my plans, just adjusting the time-frame," she told him.

"In that case, I'd appreciate those extra hands."

"I guess we'd better get the babies washed up and changed for their big photo shoot." She lifted Katie out of her high chair first. "And Jamie—"

He glanced up as he unfastened the sticky buckle around Henry's middle—evidence of the pancakes their aunt had made for them for breakfast earlier. "Yeah?"

"This is a really great idea. Fallon will love it."

He sincerely hoped his sister was right.

It was not a great idea.
In fact, it was a terrible idea.

Jamie cruised around the parking lot looking for a vacant space. Anywhere. But it was as if every single resident of Kalispell had decided to come to the mall today—and many more from neighboring towns, too.

"There," Bella said, pointing toward a woman and her daughter, both loaded down with shopping bags, who were making their way across the parking lot.

He paused in the middle of the lane, then crawled along behind them, putting his indicator on as a sign to other drivers that their parking spot—wherever it might be—was his.

It took the woman forever to load up her parcels, get into the car, and buckle her seatbelt. Then God only knows what she was doing, because she sure as hell didn't hurry to leave. Maybe she was fiddling with the radio, maybe she was programming a GPS or making a phone call. It took her two full minutes to finally decide to put her vehicle into Reverse and ease out of her narrow space.

As Jamie unfolded the triple stroller, Bella started to unbuckle the babies from their car seats so they could be loaded into their wheeled carriage and buckled up again. He was definitely grateful for her extra set of hands.

Thankfully Santa had a lot more patience than Jamie did.

Bella occupied the kids, who were now hungry and cranky, while he stood beside one of the elves to select from the digital images on the computer screen. Jamie was hungry and cranky by now, too, and tempted to walk away without a picture because none of them was the perfect shot he'd wanted for Fallon.

On the other hand, the one with Jared smiling at the camera was pretty good—even if Katie was looking in the opposite direction. But none of them was screaming and there were no tears and they were all wearing the cute little outfits she'd bought for them.

Okay, he'd forgotten Katie's shoes, so she was wearing her snow boots on her feet, and there was a wet spot on Jared's vest, where he'd spit up while they were waiting in line, and Henry's cowlick refused to be flattened. So it wasn't a perfect picture, but it perfectly captured his kids and he was confident that Fallon would love it.

When the picture had been finally printed and Bella had helped him pick a suitable frame, they went to the food court to get some French fries for the kids to nibble on while they waited for Hudson, who'd got caught in a meeting in Rust Creek Falls.

"So what kind of cake do you want?" Jamie asked his sister, when they'd found a vacant table and had finally sat down.

She smiled at him. "It's enough that you're going to walk me down the aisle—you don't have to pretend to be interested in any of the other details."

"My interest in cake is not a pretense," he told her.

"I'm thinking three or four layers, each one a different flavor—and yes, one will be chocolate."

"I want my piece cut from that layer."

"I'll make sure of it," she promised.

"So you're really going to marry this guy?"

She nodded. "I want to spend every day of the rest of my life with Hudson."

Jamie nibbled on a fry before he asked, "How did you do it?"

"What did I do?"

"Let yourself fall in love again."

His sister smiled. "I didn't 'let' myself fall in love,"

she told him. "I did, finally, let go of all the heartache from my past, and then the falling in love just happened."

"I don't think I can let go," he said. "And I feel like an idiot admitting that to you, because you've experienced as much heartache as I have."

"I'm not saying it was easy, but it was necessary," Bella said gently.

"Everyone I've ever loved has gone away." He heard the depth of emotion in his voice, and was shocked by its intensity.

"I'm still here," his sister said, as she put her hand over his. "And Fallon will be back in a few days."

"Where is she?" he asked again.

"It doesn't matter where she is now. What matters is that she'll be back."

He wasn't convinced, but he let that topic drop. Instead, he brought up another subject that had been bothering him of late. "Do you ever think about Gramps?"

"Not if I can help it," she admitted.

"You don't think we abandoned him?"

Bella frowned. "Really? You can actually ask that question after everything *he* did? He made his choices long before either of us was even born when he turned his only daughter—our mother—out of her home because she was pregnant."

"I know. But then Mom and Dad got married, and they had a great life together," he pointed out.

"Until they died," his sister said bluntly, bitterly.

He nodded, a silent acknowledgment that the car accident that had taken the lives of Rob and Lauren Stockton had significantly altered the lives of their seven children, as well.

Bella's cell buzzed and she glanced at the screen. "Hudson's here—and he's illegally parked so I've gotta run."

Jamie nodded.

She gave him a brief hug, then dropped quick kisses on the top of each of the babies' heads as she made her way past them.

"Chocolate," Jamie reminded her.

She responded with a nod and a grin before she disappeared into the crowd.

By the time he pulled into the driveway of The Short Hills Ranch and parked in front of the house, he was exhausted. Physically, from wrestling the kids in and out of their stroller, and emotionally, as a result of the conversation he'd had with his sister afterward. Of course, as soon as he turned off the ignition, all three children—who had slept in their car seats all the way from Kalispell to Rust Creek Falls—woke up, and now they were eager to play.

Since they were already bundled into their snowsuits, he decided to let them roll around in the snow for a while, opening the house to let Andy and Molly come outside to play with them.

Babies need fresh air and exercise.

His mother's voice, from so long ago, echoed in the back of his mind.

Apparently Fallon subscribed to the same idea, because he'd often seen her outside with HJK. Even when they were infants, she'd put them in their carrier or stroller or sleigh—depending on the weather—to ensure they had some outdoor time.

And there she was again—not just on his mind but

in his heart. Of course, she'd been a steady presence in his life for a lot of years, so maybe it was inevitable that he would think about her, about how it had felt to hold her, kiss her, love her.

And he did love her, but he'd been too much of a coward to admit his feelings to her. It was hard enough acknowledging the truth to himself, and his brief marriage had taught him that love wasn't a magical cure-all. Because he had loved Paula, but he'd made a lot of mistakes in their relationship.

He wasn't just afraid of making another mistake with Fallon. He was afraid of losing her forever. Ironically, it was that fear that had caused him to push her away.

But he trusted that she would be back. Not just because Bella had said so, and not even because Fallon had promised that she wouldn't abandon him, but because his heart told him that it was true.

And this time, he was going to listen to his heart.

Fallon had told him that she'd be gone a few days.

A few days wasn't so long—or so Jamie tried to convince himself.

But a few days without any word from Fallon felt like an eternity. On the fourth day, he stopped by her parents' ranch.

"Jamie—hi." Fallon's mother's greeting was pleasant enough, though she was obviously surprised to see him.

"Hi, Mrs. O'Reilly. Is Fallon here?"

"No, she isn't," Maureen said. "Didn't she tell you that she was going away?"

"She did," he confirmed. "But I thought she would be home by now."

"When I talked to her this morning, she was still in Oregon."

Oregon? "What's she doing there?" he wondered aloud.

"A personal errand," Fallon's mother said, a response that sounded deliberately vague to him.

But Jamie took solace in the fact that she didn't seem concerned about her daughter's whereabouts. "Did she say when she'd be back?"

Maureen rubbed her hands briskly up and down her arms to warm them. "It seems silly to have a conversation standing on the porch in this cold weather," she said. "Did you want to come in for a cup of coffee?"

"Coffee sounds good," he told her.

She moved away from the door so that he could enter. As soon as he stepped inside, a wriggling bundle of gold fur pounced on his boot and attacked the laces.

"Leave it, Duchess," Maureen admonished.

But Jamie only chuckled as he crouched to give the pup a scratch. "There's no doubt she's related to mine," he said. "They like to chew on anything they can sink their teeth into."

"She needs a close eye at this stage, but she's been a wonderful addition to the family."

"I was happy to hear that Brooks found good homes for all of the pups—and so quickly."

"I can't bear to think what might have happened if you hadn't found them," Maureen said, making her way to the kitchen with Duchess trotting along happily at her heels.

She took two mugs from a cupboard and filled them both with steaming brew from the carafe. "Is your sister watching your little ones this morning?"

"Yes. She was taking them to the day care, so that they could see what it's all about before they show up for their first day."

"Fallon mentioned that they were going to be starting at Just Us Kids soon," Maureen said. "Cream or sugar?"

He shook his head. "Black works for me."

She handed him one of the mugs and doctored the other for herself. He waited to sit until she had done so.

"This must be a bittersweet time for you," Maureen noted, not unkindly. "The triplets' first Christmas—and your first without your wife."

"I thought it would be," he agreed. "But I'm trying to focus on the good stuff, on making this holiday a memorable one for the kids. Of course, Fallon has been a big part of that."

"She loves the holidays—and children—so she'd want to do everything possible to help make this Christmas special for them."

"It's not just the holidays, though," he admitted. "I don't think I would have made it through the past ten months without Fallon."

"I know she's spent a lot of time with your children, but one of the greatest benefits of living in a close community like Rust Creek Falls is that neighbors always do step up to help neighbors. If Fallon hadn't been there, someone else would have been."

"I'm getting the impression you wish someone else had been," he noted.

"My youngest daughter sometimes gives too much of herself with little regard for what it may cost her," she confided.

Jamie suspected she wasn't just referring to Fallon's help with Henry, Jared and Katie.

"She's an incredible woman," he said sincerely. "And I think, for a long time, our friendship prevented me from appreciating how truly incredible."

"Are you telling me that you do now?" Maureen asked him.

He nodded. "I don't just appreciate her—I'm in love with her."

"Oh." For a moment, Fallon's mother seemed at a loss for words. Then her lips curved, just a little, into the same half smile he'd seen countless times on her daughter's face. "I have to admit, this is surprising, but not unwelcome, news."

"I hope Fallon feels the same way when I tell her," he said worriedly.

"You haven't told her?"

"By the time I realized how I felt, she was probably halfway to Oregon," he admitted.

"Well, she'll be back before Saturday," Maureen assured him. "Because it's Paddy's and my thirtieth anniversary on Christmas Eve and there's no way she'd miss that."

"No, she wouldn't," he agreed.

"We're hosting an open house to celebrate—and I know Fallon would be happy to have you and your family join us."

"Thank you," he said, grateful for the invitation and already planning how to make the most of the opportunity she'd given him.

Chapter Fourteen

When she got behind the wheel of her SUV and drove away from Rust Creek Falls, Fallon only expected to be gone a few days. But what had been intended as a three-day journey had turned into four, then five. Now on the sixth day, she was finally on her way home again.

In the past six days, she hadn't spoken to Jamie at all. He'd called, left voice mail messages and sent numerous texts, but she hadn't responded to any of them. Not because she was mad or trying to punish him for dumping her—though she still wasn't very happy about that—but because she was concerned that any communication on her part might somehow reveal the surprise she'd planned for him.

As she drove past the familiar Welcome to Rust Creek Falls sign, the excited anticipation that had fueled her through most of the long journey turned into knots of apprehension in her belly.

It wouldn't be very much longer now before she found out whether following her heart had been a brilliant move or a big mistake.

It was December 23 and Fallon still hadn't returned to Rust Creek Falls.

She hadn't even returned any of Jamie's phone calls or text messages. He wasn't worried about her—he knew that she was in contact with her family—but he was worried about *them*.

The last time he'd talked to her, he'd stupidly told her that he just wanted to be friends. She'd said she needed some time to think. What if she'd decided that he was right and that it was better for them to be friends than lovers?

The possibility tortured his mind during the day and kept him awake at night.

"You look like hell," Bella said, when he came in from the barn for lunch.

"I didn't sleep very well last night," he admitted. Or the night before, and the night before that. In fact, he'd barely slept since Fallon had abruptly left Rust Creek Falls without a word to him about where she was going or when she would be back.

"Were the babies up?" Bella asked.

He shook his head. "No, they've slept through for the past several nights."

"So why didn't you?"

"I'm worried about Fallon," he admitted.

"She'll be back today," his sister assured him.

"How do you know?"

"I spoke to her briefly this morning," she said.

"You talked to her?"

"I've talked to her—or at least texted her—almost every day since she's been gone."

He was relieved to know that Bella had been in communication with Fallon—and frustrated that his sister had deliberately withheld that information from him.

"She hasn't answered any of my calls or replied to any of my text messages," he confided.

"And why is that?" Bella wondered aloud.

He scowled. "I'm sure you know why."

"If I had to guess, I'd say it probably has something to do with the fact that you slept with her—then told her you just wanted to be friends."

He winced at the accusation in her tone. "She told you that?"

"She's my best friend—and I thought she was one of yours, too."

"I was an idiot," he admitted.

"I'm not going to argue with that," she said.

"There's no excuse for my actions, but there is an explanation. But how can I explain to Fallon if she won't even talk to me?"

"She'll listen to you," Bella told him.

"How do you know?"

"Because she's not the type to hold a grudge, and because she cares about you too much to not want to mend the rift between you."

"I hope you're right."

"I am right," she insisted. "And that's her vehicle coming up the driveway now."

He was out of the house almost before she finished speaking, without even pausing to grab his hat or jacket.

Fallon had barely shifted into park when Jamie yanked open the driver's side door and hauled her out of the SUV and into his arms. Though he squeezed all of the air from her lungs, she didn't complain. For the past six days and nights, she'd dreamed of being in his arms just like this.

You deserve someone who can give you what you want...and that's not going to be me.

With those words echoing in the back of her mind, she forced herself to pull back and deliberately kept her tone light and friendly when she said, "Do you greet all your friends this way when they return after a few days out of town?"

His arms still around her, he tipped his head down to rest his forehead against hers. "You're so much more to me than a friend," he admitted gruffly. "You're the woman who owns my heart."

Her own heart skipped a beat. "I am?" she asked cautiously.

He nodded. "I was a fool and a coward, unwilling to recognize and admit the truth of my feelings, but I'm telling you now. I love you, Fallon."

She'd almost given up hope that he would ever say those words to her and, hearing them now, she was swamped by such a wave of emotion she couldn't speak—she couldn't even breathe.

"Say something, please," he urged when she remained silent. "Tell me I'm not too late—that denying my feelings for so long didn't ruin my chance with you."

"You didn't ruin anything," she finally said. "I love you, too. I think I always have. I know I always will."

He kissed her then, with an intensity and purpose that told her even more than his words that the feelings he'd professed were real.

"Don't ever leave me like that again," he said, when he finally eased his lips from hers.

"I didn't—I wouldn't—leave you," she promised.

"It felt like you'd left me," he said. "And I don't ever want to feel so empty and alone again."

As he was talking to her, she registered the sound of another car door opening, and then closing. She pulled back, just a little, her cheeks flushing. "You almost made me forget the whole purpose of my trip," she chided gently.

But he still didn't look away from her. It was almost as if he didn't want to take his eyes off her for a single second in case she disappeared again. "You didn't just go away to punish me for being an idiot?"

"I didn't go away to punish you at all," she said, extricating herself from his embrace. "And I brought you back a present."

"You're the only present I need," Jamie assured her.

But he turned then, to follow the direction of her gaze, and was surprised to see another woman—young and blonde—standing on the other side of the car. Though she was bundled up in a long coat with a knit cap on her head, there was something vaguely familiar about her, something that stirred long ago memories buried in the back of his mind.

He sucked in a lungful of icy air as that vague familiarity shifted to hopeful recognition. But still, he was afraid to let himself believe—

"Hi, Jamie."

Her voice, when she spoke, was cautious but familiar, confirming his own tentative hope.

"Dana?" he said, speaking the name of his youngest sister who had been turned over to the child welfare authorities to be adopted more than eleven years earlier, when she was barely eight years old.

The name sounded rusty on his lips after so long, but it was all she needed to propel herself forward. And then she was in his arms. When she'd left Rust Creek Falls, she'd been a child and now she was a young woman, but holding her somehow felt the same. And so did the love that filled his heart to overflowing. Apparently he wasn't the only one feeling a little overwhelmed, because Dana clung to him as she wept. He looked over his sister's head toward Fallon, and though his mind was swirling with questions that needed answering, for now he was content to mouth a silent "thank you."

She just nodded, her own eyes bright with unshed tears.

After another moment, Dana pulled back. "I'm sorry. I promised myself that I wouldn't bawl like the baby you probably remember me to be, but I just couldn't help myself. I've missed you—all of you—every single day since I was taken away."

"I've missed you, too," he told her.

"Is Bella here?" Dana asked. "Fallon said that I'd get to see her, too."

"She's inside," Jamie said. "Which means the babies must be keeping her busy, because if she'd even peeked out the window and caught a glimpse of you, I know she'd be out here, too."

"Fallon showed me pictures of your triplets, and I can't wait to meet them."

"Then let's go inside so you can." He started toward the house, but turned back when he realized Fallon wasn't beside him. "Bella and the babies will want to see you, too."

But she shook her head. "We'll catch up later. I don't want to intrude on your family reunion."

"Which wouldn't be happening at all, if not for you," he pointed out.

"My sisters have been texting me nonstop for three days, sending me lists of all the things we need to do before our parents' anniversary party tomorrow."

He didn't want to let her go, but he understood that she had things she needed to do—and that she'd fallen behind schedule because she'd gone out of town for him, to give him back a piece of his family.

"Okay," he finally relented. "But I'll see you tomorrow."

"I'm counting on it," she said.

He hugged her again. "I want to know how and why, but for now, I'll just say thank you."

"The how is kind of complicated," she admitted. "But the why is simple—I wanted you to know that even when the people we love go away, the love endures."

Jamie didn't know if he could process all of the thoughts and feelings that were clamoring for prominence inside him.

Of course he'd thought about tracking down his siblings. Over the years, he'd thought about it a lot. Reconnecting with his brothers and sisters was something he'd dreamed about ever since the day they were separated.

But in the past year, the idea had been shoved to the back of the mind. With so many other and much more immediate concerns, he hadn't let himself think about or miss his other siblings. Or maybe that was just an excuse. Because the truth was, Luke, Daniel and Bailey had chosen to go off on their own. They knew where

Jamie and Bella had been living with their grandparents and they'd chosen to let eleven years pass without making contact in all of that time.

But Dana and Liza had been taken away and he didn't know where they'd ended up. Again, he would have expected they were old enough to remember the time they'd spent in Rust Creek Falls, but after they'd gone, they'd never made any attempt to communicate with him and Bella.

And now, after all of that time, Dana was here. Not through her own initiative and not because of any effort on his part, but because Fallon had tracked her down and brought her to Rust Creek Falls. He didn't know how long Dana would stay—or could stay—but she was here now. Fallon had brought one of his little sisters home, and he knew he wouldn't ever be able to repay her.

He thought about what she'd said—the words she'd whispered in his ear when she'd hugged him. *Even when the people we love go away, the love endures.*

She'd proven that to him twice today—by bringing his sister to Rust Creek Falls and by coming back herself. And now that she was finally home, he was going to do everything in his power to ensure that she never wanted to leave again.

Fallon was up early the next morning to help Fiona and Brenna with the hors d'oeuvres. Her hands went through the necessary motions, but her mind—and her heart—were at The Short Hills Ranch with Jamie.

Jamie. She felt her lips curve as she thought of the man who had held her in his arms as if he never wanted to let her go. The man who had kissed her as if he wanted to kiss her forever. The man who had told her—finally—that he loved her.

Fiona snapped her fingers in front of her face. "Earth to Fallon. We're expecting upwards of a hundred guests between four and seven, which means that we're going to need a lot of meatballs, sausage rolls, shrimp skewers, pinwheel sandwiches, vegetable crudités, platters of cheeses and crackers and fruit, and I need your attention on this planet."

Fallon resumed her chopping. The girls were in charge of the food and the boys were in charge of the setup, which meant rearranging the furniture to accommodate the folding tables and chairs borrowed from the community center, and all the while Duchess was running around, doing her best to trip up everyone as they performed their assigned tasks.

Surrounded by her family—whom she loved with every fiber of her being despite the fact that they often drove her crazy—it was natural that her thoughts would drift to Jamie and Bella, that she would wonder how the reunion with Dana was going. She'd been relieved to witness the success of the initial meeting, pleased that the siblings were happy to be together again after so many years. But Fallon knew that a lot had happened during the time they'd been apart and it was possible that, when all the tales had been told, old wounds would be reopened and tender feelings hurt.

"Fallon—" it was Ronan who interrupted her musing this time "—can you give me a hand with these chairs?"

"Where's Keegan?" she asked.

"I sent him to pick up the flowers and balloons."

"Mistake," Brenna told their oldest brother.

"Why?"

"He had a total of three things to pick up at Crawford's yesterday and he forgot one of them," Fiona piped in.

"Although I don't think he actually forgot," Brenna said. "I think he wanted an excuse to go back and flirt with Natalie Crawford."

"I don't care how much flirting he does as long as he's back with the balloons and flowers before Mom and Dad get home," Ronan said.

"Where are they?" Fallon asked.

"Mom went to Bee's Beauty Parlor to get her hair done and Dad's on his way back from Kalispell."

"Why did he have to go into the city today?" Brenna asked.

"Probably to find an anniversary present for Mom," Fallon guessed.

"To pick up her anniversary present," Ronan clarified. "A strand of Akoya pearls."

"Pearls are the traditional gift for a thirtieth anniversary," Fiona noted.

Fallon nodded. "And Mom's always wanted real pearls."

"Well, I guess Dad decided that thirty years was long enough to wait," Ronan said.

"She's going to cry," Fiona warned.

Fallon's own eyes were a little moist as she imagined Maureen's reaction to the gift, as she considered how it might feel to be part of a couple that had endured for three decades. No, not just endured but flourished.

"What did Mom get for Dad?" Brenna wondered.

"Super Bowl tickets," Fiona told her.

Fallon laughed. "Not traditional, but definitely something Dad's always wanted."

"Which just goes to show how perfectly suited they are for one another," Brenna said.

"Put the sentiment on hold until the party," Ronan advised. "The clock is ticking."

As a result of her oldest brother's constant prompting and nagging, everything was set up and ready for the party when the guests of honor got home. Since she hadn't really had a chance to talk to her mother since her trip to Oregon, Fallon offered to help Maureen get changed.

"You look beautiful," Fallon said, after she'd zipped up the back of her mother's dress.

"Bee has a knack with hair," her mother said.

She shook her head. "Your hair looks nice, but it's more than that. You're glowing." And she knew it was love that put the color in Maureen's cheeks and the sparkle in her eyes. Not just being in love but knowing that she was loved in return. Fallon suspected that she had a little bit of a glow herself and wondered if her mother could see it.

Maureen laughed softly. "I've been reminiscing a lot today," she admitted. "Paddy and I have made a lot of memories together over thirty years and five children."

"You've definitely shown us what a good marriage should look like," Fallon told her.

"I hope so," her mother said. "Your dad and I don't always agree about everything, but hopefully that showed our kids the importance of navigating stormy seas, the value of compromise and, at the end of the day, the necessity of working together.

"That's what I want for all of my children," Maureen continued. "An enduring lifelong partnership with someone who loves, respects and supports them."

"It doesn't sound like so much, does it?" Fallon noted wistfully. "But it's huge, and I know how lucky I am to have grown up in this family."

"You're thinking of Jamie again, aren't you?" her mom asked gently.

"Jamie, Bella, Dana and the rest of their family," she admitted.

"It was such a tragedy for all of them, losing their parents the way they did. And Agnes and Matthew—" Maureen shook her head "—I can't begin to know what they were thinking, letting the older boys go off on their own and sending the younger girls away, but I think you've helped Jamie and Bella see that even broken pieces can fit back together."

"You don't think I overstepped by bringing Dana to Rust Creek Falls?"

"I don't think it's ever wrong to follow your heart."

"I love him, Mom."

Her mother smiled. "I know you do."

"I tried not to," she admitted. "But he's it for me."

"That's how it was for me with your father," Maureen confided, lifting a hand to tuck a wayward curl behind her daughter's ear. "I'm glad you didn't straighten your hair today—I like the natural look."

"I thought I had to change to get Jamie's attention," she confessed. "But as it turns out, he likes the real me. He loves the real me."

"Because he's as smart as he is handsome," her mother remarked.

"Speaking of smart and handsome men—let's go find your husband before the guests start arriving."

It seemed as if all of the residents of Rust Creek Falls showed up to wish Paddy and Maureen O'Reilly a happy anniversary. Some folks just passed through to offer a brief "congratulations" while others settled in for a longer visit with friends and neighbors and to enjoy the food and drink provided. Even Homer Gilmore stopped by to offer his best wishes. While the old man was in the house, Fallon kept a close eye on him to ensure that he never got close enough to the punch bowl to spike the fruity drink Brenna had prepared.

It was close to five o'clock when Jamie showed up.

She hadn't been certain that he would come. She'd invited him and Bella and Dana, but she knew the three siblings had a lot of catching up to do and she wouldn't have blamed them for skipping the party.

Hudson and Bella came in first, with Bella carrying Henry. Dana followed with Jared in her arms, then Jamie walked through the door with Katie. It was readily apparent that the newly found Stockton sister had already fallen head over heels in love with her niece and nephews, and it warmed Fallon's heart to see them all together, to see that the bond they'd shared as children had not been broken by the time or distance that had separated them.

There were still four other siblings to be found, but she knew that Jamie would find them. She'd helped him take the first step; now it was time for her to step back and let the Stocktons figure out their family.

She tried to make her way to him through the crowd but was halted in her tracks when Paddy put his fingers between his lips and whistled to silence the crowd.

"Sorry to interrupt, folks, but I wanted to take a few

minutes to thank you all for coming today to celebrate our anniversary with Maureen and me."

The crowd cheered and applauded, but Paddy—an Irishman to the bone—wasn't even close to being done.

"I'd also like to make a couple of toasts," he said, "so make sure your glasses are full.

"First, and most important on this day, to my always beautiful and amazing wife. These first thirty years have been a heck of a ride, and I'm looking forward to the next three decades—and more."

The crowd applauded and cheered.

"I'd also like to toast our children who, through the many challenges they presented to us over the years, taught Maureen and me a lot about the trials and tribulations of parenting."

There was, predictably, some laughter to follow that.

"But seriously, when Maureen and I exchanged our vows, we were united in our desire not just to spend our lives together but to fill our home with children. We were fortunate to be blessed with Ronan, Keegan, Fiona, Brenna and Fallon, who have enriched our lives in more ways than we ever would have thought possible. And who will hopefully further enrich our lives by giving us the wonderful gift of grandchildren someday."

There was more laughter and the clinking of glasses again, then Fallon saw Jamie hand his daughter to Hudson and step forward. Her heart hammered against her ribs as her mind wondered, what was he doing?

"Since you brought up the topic," Jamie said, addressing her father, "I was wondering if you'd mind having your lives enriched by grandchildren sooner rather than later?"

Paddy's bushy brows lifted to meet his hairline. "I'd

guess that would depend on the circumstances," he said. "What, exactly, are you asking?"

Fallon held her breath, waiting for Jamie's response. Thankfully, he didn't make her wait long. Through the crowd, his eyes found and held hers as he said, "I'm asking for your daughter's hand in marriage."

And Fallon's heart swelled to fill her chest.

But it was Brenna who piped up to say, "And I accept."

Paddy chuckled as several other guests began to whisper about this unexpected turn of events and Jamie's face turned red.

"I guess you should have been more specific," the O'Reilly patriarch suggested.

Jamie nodded. "I would like to ask for *Fallon's* hand in marriage," he clarified.

Brenna let out an exaggerated sigh. "You're dumping me already?"

Fallon elbowed her sister sharply in the ribs as laughter sounded around the room. She couldn't imagine it had been easy for Jamie to make a public declaration of his feelings and she didn't want him to shy away now. Not when he was so close to finally asking the question she'd been waiting to hear for so long.

She looked toward her father and saw Paddy offer his hand to Jamie.

"You and your children would be a welcome addition to the family," he said, then he raised his glass again. "And now we have another reason to celebrate today— not just an anniversary but an engagement."

Everyone cheered again.

Everyone except Fallon who, when the murmur of the crowd died down, finally spoke up. Because while the moment was pretty close to being perfect, she still wanted an actual proposal. "I'm pleased to see that everyone is having a good time, but I think some of this revelry might be a little premature."

"So long as he's not…premature…in the bedroom," Winona Cobbs piped up.

Which, of course, made Fallon's face turn red, but her gaze didn't shift away from Jamie.

He took a ring out of his pocket, lowered himself to one knee in front of her and finally offered her what she most wanted in the world—and it wasn't a diamond in a band of gold, it was his heart. "Fallon, will you do me the honor of becoming my wife?"

Her eyes misted and her heart, already full, overflowed with love and happiness. "I feel as if I've been waiting my whole life for you to ask me that question," she confessed.

"Is that a yes?" Keegan interjected. "Because when a guy asks a yes-or-no question, he just wants a yes-or-no answer."

"And he'd probably appreciate the rest of her family butting out so that she can answer the question," Fiona said pointedly.

Fallon continued to hold Jamie's gaze as she shook her head in response to her family's antics. "I'll bet you're regretting the public proposal now, aren't you?"

"My only regret would be if you said no," he told her sincerely. "Because I don't want anything so much as I want to spend the rest of my life with you."

"Yes," she finally said. "My answer is yes, because I want exactly the same thing."

He took her hand but paused with the ring—a stunning princess-cut diamond solitaire—at the tip of her finger. "You do understand that marrying me will mean becoming an instant mother to three adorable, messy and demanding children?"

"I do," she agreed. "And I love those adorable, messy and demanding children every bit as much as I love you."

He smiled and slid the ring onto her finger.

"I love you, Fallon O'Reilly," he said, whispering the words against her lips.

"And I love you, Jamie Stockton."

And then, finally, he kissed her.

"Well, it's official," Jamie said, dropping onto the sofa beside his fiancée and surveying the disaster zone that had once been his living room.

In the middle of the floor littered with discarded paper, Henry was trying to pull off his socks, Katie was banging on a drum, Jared was collecting all the green bows—and only the green ones—in a toy shopping cart, Molly was chewing on a red bow and Andy, apparently worn out from all of the excitement, was sprawled on his back beneath the Christmas tree.

On the coffee table were two framed photos: similar but different pictures of the babies with Santa, one wrapped up for Jamie by Fallon and the other for Fallon by Jamie. They'd both had a good chuckle over that.

Fallon tipped her head back against his shoulder. "What's official?"

"This was undoubtedly The. Best. Christmas. Ever."

She smiled. "Only until next Christmas," she promised.

"Well, while we're still celebrating *this* Christmas, I have one more gift for you."

She took the small, flat package and peeled away the paper, then opened the lid of the box to reveal a silver snowflake ornament decorated with sparkling crystals.

"It's beautiful," she said.

"Turn it over."

She did as he suggested and found that it was inscribed on the back with a date and the words: Fallon & Jamie—First Christmas Together.

"I love it," she said, softly, sincerely.

"The first of many," he told her.

"I'm already looking forward to each and every one," she assured him.

"I'm hoping that next Christmas I'll get to wake up with you in my arms."

Because although they were engaged, engaged wasn't married, and Paddy and Maureen had made it clear that they expected their unmarried daughter to wake up under their roof and spend Christmas morning with her family. Which she had done, then she'd come over to The Short Hills Ranch to celebrate with Jamie and the babies.

"Me, too," she said.

"Does that mean you're ready to set a date for our wedding?"

"We haven't even been engaged twenty-four hours," she pointed out.

"Is there some kind of required waiting period that I don't know about?" he teased.

"I just thought you might want to wait until all of your brothers and sisters could be at our wedding."

But he shook his head. "I want to find them—I *am* going to find them—but I have no idea how long that's going to take and I'm not willing to put our wedding on hold until it happens." He kissed her softly. "Because I want to spend every day of the rest of my life with you, and I want the rest of our life together to start as soon as possible."

"That sounds like a perfect plan to me," she agreed.

Epilogue

Three months later

"That's a lot of cupcakes," Jamie commented, looking at the miniature frosted cakes that had been assembled on the table to spell out Happy 1st Birthday.

"There are a lot of babies celebrating today," Fallon reminded him.

Although Henry, Jared and Katie had celebrated their birthday two months earlier, they'd been invited to this party, along with everyone else in town, to celebrate the first anniversary of the Baby Bonanza—as many residents had taken to calling the population explosion that had occurred nine months after Braden and Jennifer's Fourth of July wedding.

"They look like they're all vanilla," he said, sounding disappointed.

"There's leftover chocolate cake in your fridge from the bakery that's going to make our wedding cake," she reminded him.

They'd decided on May twentieth as the date for their wedding, because it gave them a few months to make the arrangements and would allow them to take time for a honeymoon before Bella and Hudson exchanged their vows.

Maureen had initially been a little concerned that they were rushing their nuptials, but Fallon assured her mother that she didn't feel rushed at all. She'd been in love with Jamie since she was seventeen years old and she was excited about finally starting their life together.

"I can see now why so many women who want to have babies believe there's something in the water in Rust Creek Falls," Fallon commented, as more families and more babies entered the community center for the celebration.

"Except it wasn't the water but the wedding punch," Jamie reminded her. "I'm not sure if Homer Gilmore should be given the key to the city or put in jail and the key thrown away."

"No doubt that's a topic that has been widely debated around town, but I'd vote for the key to the city," Fallon said. "Because if it wasn't for Homer spiking the wedding punch, we wouldn't have Henry, Jared and Katie."

"True," he acknowledged. "But when we decide to expand our family again, I'd be content to let nature take its course."

It was the first time he'd mentioned having another child, and Fallon was both pleased and surprised. "You want to have another child?"

"I'm not in any hurry," he assured her. "Especially

considering that we aren't married yet and already have three babies in diapers. But I loved growing up with so many brothers and sisters, and I'd be thrilled to add to our family in a couple of years."

"I'd like that, too," she told him. "But I really hope we grow our family one baby at a time."

"How would you feel if you did end up pregnant with twins or triplets?" he asked curiously.

She looked at Henry, Jared and Katie, playing with the toys that had been scattered in the middle of the room, and thought back to the early days when they'd been so tiny and fragile and demanding. The first few months had been incredibly hard, and there had been days when she'd wanted to cry right along with them. But for every one of those days, there were countless more during which she'd felt nothing but pure and un-adulterated joy simply because Henry rolled over or Jared clapped his hands or Katie smiled at her— simply because they were a part of her life. And that was even before they'd stopped calling her 'Fa-fa' in favor of 'Ma-ma.'

"Blessed," she finally responded to his question. "I would feel doubly or triply blessed."

He smiled and slid an arm across her shoulders. "Let's gather up our kids and go get some cupcakes."

* * * * *

#2521 A FORTUNE IN WAITING
The Fortunes of Texas: The Secret Fortunes • by Michelle Major
Everyone in Austin is charmed by architect Keaton Fortune Whitfield, the sexy new British Fortune in town—except Francesca Harriman, waitress at Lola May's and the one woman he wants in his life! Can he win the heart of the beautiful hometown girl?

#2522 TWICE A HERO, ALWAYS HER MAN
Matchmaking Mamas • by Marie Ferrarella
When popular news reporter Elliana King interviews Colin Benteen, a local police detective, she had no idea this was the man who tried to save her late husband's life—nor did she realize that he would capture her heart.

#2523 THE COWBOY'S RUNAWAY BRIDE
Celebration, TX • by Nancy Robards Thompson
Lady Chelsea Ashford Alden was forced to flee London after her fiancé betrayed her, and now seeks refuge with her best friend in Celebration. When Ethan Campbell catches her climbing in through a window, he doesn't realize the only thing Chelsea will be stealing is his heart...

#2524 THE MAKEOVER PRESCRIPTION
Sugar Falls, Idaho • by Christy Jeffries
Baseball legend Kane Chatterson has tried hard to fly under the radar since his epic scandal—until a beautiful society doctor named Julia Fitzgerald comes along and throws him a curveball! She may be a genius, but men were never her strong suit. Who better than the former MVP of the dating scene to help her out?

#2525 WINNING THE NANNY'S HEART
The Barlow Brothers • by Shirley Jump
When desperate widower Sam Millwright hires Katie Williams to be his nanny, he finds a way back to his kids—and a second chance at love.

#2526 HIS BALLERINA BRIDE
Drake Diamonds • by Teri Wilson
Former ballerina and current jewelry designer Ophelia Rose has caught the eye of the new CEO of Drake Diamonds, Artem Drake, but she has more secrets than the average woman. A kitten, the ballet and *lots* of diamonds might just help these two lonely souls come together in glitzy, snowy New York City.

"The dog wasn't the silver lining." He tapped one finger on the top of the box. "You and pie are the silver lining. I hope you have time to have a piece with me." He leaned in. "You know it's bad luck to eat pie alone."

She made a sound that was half laugh and half sigh. "That might explain some of the luck I've had in life. I hate to admit the amount of pie I've eaten on my own."

His heart twisted as a pain she couldn't quite hide flared in those caramel eyes. His well-honed protective streak kicked in, but it was also more than that. He wanted to take up the sword and go to battle against whatever dragons had hurt this lovely, vibrant woman.

It was an idiotic notion, both because Francesca had never given him any indication that she needed assistance slaying dragons and because he didn't have the genetic makeup of a hero. Not with Gerald Robinson as his father.

But he couldn't quite make himself walk away from the chance to give her what he could that might once again put a smile on her beautiful face.

"Then it's time for a dose of good luck." He stepped back and pulled out a chair at the small, scuffed conference table in the center of the office. "I can't think of a better way to begin than with a slice of Pick-Me-Up Pecan Pie. Join me?"

Her gaze darted to the door before settling on him. "Yes, thank you," she murmured and dropped into the seat.

Her scent drifted up to him—vanilla and spice, perfect for the type of woman who would bake a pie from scratch. He'd never considered baking to be a particularly sexy activity, but the thought of Francesca wearing an apron in the kitchen as she mixed ingredients for his pie made sparks dance across his skin.

The mental image changed to Francesca wearing nothing but an apron and—

"I have plates," he shouted and she jerked back in the chair.

"That's helpful," she answered quietly, giving him a curious look. "Do you have forks, too?"

"Yes, forks." He turned toward the small bank of cabinets installed in one corner of the trailer. "And napkins," he called over his shoulder. Damn, he sounded like a complete prat.

Don't miss
A FORTUNE IN WAITING by Michelle Major,
available January 2017 wherever
Harlequin® Special Edition books and ebooks are sold.

www.Harlequin.com

HARLEQUIN®

A *Romance* FOR EVERY MOOD™

JUST CAN'T GET ENOUGH?

Join our social communities
and talk to us online.

You will have access to the latest
news on upcoming titles and special
promotions, but most importantly,
you can talk to other fans about your
favorite Harlequin reads.

Harlequin.com/Community

 Facebook.com/HarlequinBooks

 Twitter.com/HarlequinBooks

Pinterest.com/HarlequinBooks

THE WORLD IS BETTER WITH

Romance

Harlequin has everything from contemporary, passionate and heartwarming to suspenseful and inspirational stories.

Whatever your mood, we have romance when you need it, wherever you are!

⬥ HARLEQUIN®

A *Romance* FOR EVERY MOOD™

www.Harlequin.com

#RomanceWhenYouNeedIt